The Incident at
Wheeler's Canyon

It sounded easy. Escort two nuns and five Mexican orphans across the desert to foster parents in the town of Northend. What could go wrong? Or so thinks Zachary Cobb of Bellington's private detective agency.

Before he and his companion even meet the group, they are attacked and the children are kidnapped and held for ransom by the ruthless Kelman gang. Now, with the dubious help of Sister Mary Joseph, it is up to Cobb to rescue them.

In this rip-roaring yarn of the old West, the action never stops for a moment and the reader will be hooked from beginning to end.

The Incident at Wheeler's Canyon

STEVEN GRAY

A Black Horse Western

ROBERT HALE · LONDON

Typeset by
Derek Doyle & Associates, Liverpool.
Printed and bound in Great Britain by
Antony Rowe Limited, Wiltshire

ONE

Santa Fe, New Mexico. It should have been easy. Ride in, rob the bank, ride out. They'd done the same numerous times before. Successfully.

The Kelman Gang, led by Kenny Kelman, who was usually a good leader and a good planner, had always been successful; no serious injuries amongst the men, never in danger of capture by the law, a vast haul of cash. Now two of them had been shot to death on the dusty street and instead of having pockets full of dollars they were running from the law having stolen hardly anything. Kelman couldn't understand what had gone wrong. But gone wrong it had. And he didn't like the feeling of failure.

'They still coming after us?' Brad Worley asked.

Everyone else keeping well out of his way, Kelman walked to the edge of the small camp they'd made and looked at their back trail. He was just turned twenty-eight. A tall, thin man with black hair hanging in braids to his shoulders and a whiskery chin. Hard brown eyes to go with his hard nature. In the distance, a long way off but there nevertheless, was a rise of dust – the damn posse. Why didn't the marshal just give up like all the marshals before him?

'Yeah. Best get the others ready to ride out.'

'They won't like it,' Worley went on in warning, as if Kelman needed warning. 'They're all tired and hungry.'

'They'll like getting caught damn well less,' Kelman said angrily, thinking he was tired too with being responsible for the rest when all they did was complain.

'OK,' Worley said, knowing better than to argue.

The two men had been friends for years. Worley was the only man Kelman liked or trusted. And Worley liked Kenny even though he was wary of the man's quick and uncertain temper. They'd met in a town jail, waiting trial for causing drunken mayhem. They found they had a lot in common. Both came from West Texas. Both were the sons of poor dirt farmers with never enough money to go round. Both had decided, early on, that they didn't want the same sort of life, which wasn't a life but only an existence.

One night, before the judge came to town, they overpowered the jailer and escaped. On the run they decided to give up the idea of becoming cowboys, turning to robbery and killing instead, which seemed so much easier than hard work. Other members of the gang had come and gone but they had stuck together.

Twenty-five, Worley was short and squat but very strong. With his fair curly hair and blue eyes, he would have been good-looking but for a puckered knife-scar disfiguring his right cheek. The wound hadn't put him off using a knife (the other man had come off much worse) and it was still his weapon of choice.

Now he looked at Kelman knowing that what had happened in Santa Fe was testing both his patience and his leadership.

It had started out all right. The eight outlaws rode into the town with no one taking any notice of them. The streets and the bank had already been scouted, the robbery planned. They left the horses on the other side of the street, guarded by Billy and Joe, and entered the bank. And that was when it all went wrong. A customer came in behind them just as they were drawing their guns. Before he could be stopped he'd run out again.

'They're robbing the bank!' his cry went up. 'Robbing the bank!'

Billy chased and grabbed him. It was too late. Those nearby were already alerted. Someone ran for the marshal. Others took up defensive positions. Billy shot the interfering busybody but then someone else shot Billy.

Even worse, in the confusion, the single bank clerk took the opportunity to dash into the manager's office. Had locked himself in.

'Now what?' Worley cried.

'Get the money in the till,' Kelman ordered.

Little enough but to get into the safe without the clerk's key and with armed citizens arriving outside would take far too long. He knew they had no choice but to get out.

Worley peeked out of the window and nearly got his head shot off. 'They're waiting for us. Hell! Kenny, what shall we do?'

'We can't stay here.'

A man had been killed, others killed in their past raids. There was a price on all their heads and they were wanted "dead or alive".

'We'll have to make a run for it!'

Gun in hand, Kelman led the charge out of the bank. Immediately, they were greeted by bullets coming at them from every direction. That was when the second gang member was shot, falling down the steps leading to the bank, leaving behind a ribbon of red.

'Come on, come on,' Kelman yelled at Joe, who was trying to drag the scared horses across the street.

Keeping in a tight circle the outlaws returned the fire. Another citizen was hit. Amidst the noise of guns and yells, the marshal arrived and let loose with a scattergun, buckshot whipping by their heads. They scrambled aboard the horses and galloped away, keeping low in the saddle as shots followed them. Even then it wasn't over. A large and determined posse gave chase, almost caught them once or twice.

And the damn posse was still there, following them.

'What the hell are we goin' to do?' Worley asked as Kelman kicked dust on the fire.

Two men dead. Not enough money to go round. Chased by a bunch of townsmen who weren't giving up. Too many of them for the gang to stop and shoot it out. It wasn't the first setback Kelman had suffered in his life but it was the most disastrous.

Now he said, 'Arizona ain't far. Just over that ridge of hills by my reckoning. We get there the damn posse will have to give up.'

'You sure?'

'Yeah.' Kelman wasn't but no way would he admit that. A good leader had always to be confident. 'And once there we can head for the desert.'

Where there would be little or no law to trouble them. And where he could plan what to do. He already had an idea in mind. It wasn't a great idea but at least nothing could go wrong with it. And afterwards they'd have time to decide what to do, where to go.

The posse came to a halt at the edge of the hills, a vast empty valley stretching out in front of them, nothing but sand and the grey-green of sagebrush.

'They've crossed into Arizona,' the marshal said.

'Can we follow 'em?'

The marshal would have liked nothing better than to catch up with the bastards who'd come into his town and shot dead two of its citizens. But he knew that once the outlaws reached the desert with its hidden arroyos and rocky outbreaks they could easily escape pursuit or set up an ambush. And unfortunately they were far enough ahead for them to reach the desert long before the posse.

Reluctantly he shook his head. 'It's no use. We'll have to turn back.'

And when they reached Santa Fe the first thing he'd do would be to send out telegraphs to warn others that the Kelman gang was likely heading their way.

'See, I done told you the posse wouldn't chase us no more,' Kelman said. 'We're safe now.'

It was over a week since they'd crossed into Arizona. Kelman had not only put the abortive raid on the bank behind him but had managed, thanks to a small hamlet they'd passed through and a telegraph operator he'd made help him and then shot, to put his plan in motion.

'You sure they'll be coming this way?' Worley asked.

'Oh yeah,' Kelman said with a grin. 'Should be quite soon.'

TWO

Nuns and children!

For once Zachary Cobb and Neil Travis were in agreement.

'The mission should be just over the hill,' Cobb said. 'Not far now.'

He and Neil looked at one another in dismay. How did you behave with nuns and children?

Cobb might have been flattered when Mr Bellington assured him he was being sent to Arizona because he was the best man for the job. He wasn't. Mr Bellington seldom flattered the private detectives who worked for his agency. Any compliments were said for a purpose. For, having been told how good he was, how could Cobb turn the job down? On the whole Cobb liked working for Mr Bellington; he certainly liked being a private detective, but this time he left the office feeling he'd been well and truly lumbered.

'What exactly is it we're going to do?' Neil asked.

'Exactly? I'm not sure.'

Mr Bellington had said, 'You're to go to the Mission of San Francisco in Arizona. Meet a Father Flynn. He wants an escort for a couple of nuns and several children from the mission to the town of Northend. He'll tell you the details.'

Now, Cobb and Neil came to a halt just below the ridge. It had been a long and hot ride from the railroad halt, where they'd hired horses, and they wanted to stretch their legs. More important, they both wanted to put off arriving at the mission. It wasn't often they were in one accord but they were as far as dealing with nuns and children was concerned.

They were a mismatched pair. Cobb was tall, wiry and strong. In keeping with his position as a private detective working for a reputable agency his dark-brown hair was cut short and he was clean-shaven. Even riding across the desert he dressed as neatly as the circumstances allowed.

Mr Bellington had a number of rules and regulations; actually he had a great many of them. One of them was that his detectives shouldn't associate with outlaws. Neil wasn't exactly an outlaw but he had been a thief and he didn't, in any way, look neat or tidy, having straggly brown hair hanging below his shoulders, a skimpy moustache and mismatched clothes. Quite why Cobb had rescued Neil from a life of crime and agreed he could accompany him, he didn't know. But he was as lumbered with Neil as he was with this job.

'I've never met a nun before,' Neil said, taking a drink of warm water from his canteen.

Nor had Cobb.

'What do I say to them?'

Cobb wasn't sure about that either but he felt a word of caution was in order. 'There must be no bad language, no bad habits or bad anything.'

Neil gave a heavy sigh. He wasn't looking forward to this one little bit.

'Never mind,' Cobb said, swinging himself up into the saddle. 'This might be a difficult job but I don't see how it can be dangerous.'

'Why not?'

'Well, who would want to hurt two nuns and a bunch of kids?'

The Mission of San Francisco was extremely old, having been first built by the Spaniards during their conquest of the West in the seventeenth century. It lay on the edge of a flat, dusty valley, ringed by low foothills, the site chosen because of a small waterhole that even in the hottest and driest of years never completely dried up and round which a grove of cottonwood trees provided welcome shade.

Once it had been surrounded by irrigated fields of maize, cultivated vegetable plots and grazing cattle: an oasis in the desert for Mexicans and friendly Pueblo Indians. Now as Cobb and Neil rode towards it they saw there were no fields, only one small vegetable garden and the livestock seemed to consist of a couple of milk cows and a few chickens pecking in the dirt. The adobe buildings – a squat church with a bell tower, the long low mission house and a few work buildings – were painted eye-achingly white and appeared in reasonably good repair.

An old Indian was working in the garden, plying a hoe to the earth. He looked up at their approach but otherwise took no notice. However, when they came to a halt in front of the mission house, a Mexican boy appeared out of nowhere to take their horses, smiling and nodding politely as he did so, and a few seconds later the door opened to reveal Father Flynn.

In his fifties, he was a large man with white hair and blue eyes contrasting with sunburnt, leathery skin. He wore a long white habit, clean for the most part but dark with dust at the bottom, and stout sandals.

'Zachary Cobb?' he said, reaching out a rough work-hardened hand for Cobb to shake. 'You've made good time. Come on in out of the sun, have some lemonade.'

'Thanks. This is Neil Travis. He's my . . . er . . . yeah.' Cobb always had difficulty in knowing how to introduce Neil.

The mission house was cool and dimly lit with tiny windows and thick doors. It consisted of one main room with a long table and benches in the middle and beyond that a corridor with other rooms – kitchen, parlour, bedrooms – leading off it. Furnishings and decorations were minimal and practical. But it was clean and dustfree and the lemonade, served by the same boy who had taken

their horses, was cold and to Neil's relief, because he was always hungry, it was accompanied by home-made biscuits.

'I expect you're wondering why I asked for Mr Bellington's help,' Father Flynn said, but although Cobb nodded it seemed he wasn't in any hurry to explain. For, with a dreamy expression in his eyes, he went on, 'I've been here almost since I was ordained. A long time ago now, when I was a young man. Probably not much older than you,' he added with a nod and smile at Neil. 'I love the land and the people, Mexican and Indian alike, but there's no doubt that both can be harsh and dangerous.'

'You are isolated here,' Cobb agreed.

'That we are. But I wasn't really talking about the mission. Most of those who live roundabout know we have their best interests at heart and apart from the hungry trying to steal a chicken or young bucks wanting to prove their manhood by firing arrows at our cows, we don't suffer much trouble.'

Cobb said nothing. He thought that with the obvious poverty of the mission, even losing a chicken, much more a milk cow, might prove difficult, if not disastrous.

'No, it's the children I'm sorry for.'

'Oh?'

'Especially the Mexican children. They're usually poor to start with, with little to look forward to except a life of more of the same. And what happens to them if their parents are killed in Indian raids or by bandits? The children are left as orphans. Some have families who care for them but some don't and they face starvation or ending up being used and abused. You know how it is, Mr Cobb.'

Cobb nodded. He knew only too well how the innocent were exploited by the unscrupulous.

Looking angry and upset, Father Flynn went on, 'I'm afraid that's the fate of most. But we do manage to save a few, a very few.'

'How?' Neil asked, mouth full of biscuit, earning himself a glare from Cobb.

'They are taken to a nunnery in California. There they will be treated for their ills, physical and mental, and receive perhaps the first kindness of their lives. They're fed and clothed and when they're better some are found suitable foster parents.' Father Flynn paused for a moment. 'Unfortunately that's not always possible. The children are perhaps too distressed by their experiences to respond to help. They might be badly ill or crippled. Or maybe the people who come forward to claim them aren't suitable. We have to be very careful as to whom they're placed with and who we place. It's no use raising false hopes on either side.'

'What happens to those you can't help?'

'They either stay at the nunnery or depending on their condition go to hospitals or orphanages. All good places but no substitute for a loving home.'

Cobb glanced across at Neil. He could never be said to have enjoyed a loving home, living as he had with a bully of a father and a worse bully of a brother – which come to think of it was the reason he'd agreed to let Neil accompany him. He resolved, not for the first time, to behave better towards Neil in the future.

'And you try to find these suitable foster parents?'

'Yes. Of course I'm not the only one. And believe me it's not easy because most families have a hard enough struggle feeding their own children and don't want to take on any more.' Father Flynn too glanced at Neil who had eaten most of the biscuits. 'But after a long search four families in and near to the town of Northend have been found who are willing to take in five children, all the arrangements being made with Paul Drummond, Northend's mayor.'

'So you haven't actually seen these families?'

'No.'

'How do you know they're suitable?'

Father Flynn smiled. 'Sister Mary Joseph is in charge of that side of things.'

Sister Mary Joseph? Neil wondered how someone could have both a female and male name. 'She's one of the nuns?'

'That's right. She and Sister Catherine are accompanying the children. It's not the first time Sister Mary Joseph has done this sort of thing. Believe me she'll be able to tell whether these families are on the level or not! And woe betide them if they're not.'

Neil wasn't sure if he liked the sound of that. Supposing she didn't think he was suitable to ride with Cobb?

'If she's so experienced why do you need our help?'

Cobb asked, helping himself to another glass of lemonade.

'I wouldn't normally,' Father Flynn admitted. 'Northend is only a couple of days' wagon-ride away from here and although it's rough country in between it's not particularly dangerous.'

'So?'

'Well, the last couple of months we've had a bit of trouble from Indians. Nothing much but a few young Apaches decided to break out of their Reservation and head for the border. On their way through they stole a couple of our chickens and did some damage amongst the crops. I don't think they're around any more and I don't think they'd harm two nuns but I didn't like to take the chance. Even more worrying,' with a frown the man leant forward, resting his elbows on the table, 'there's meant to be an outlaw band running for the desert.'

That made Cobb interested. 'Know who they are?'

'The Kelman Gang.'

Cobb thought for a moment or two. The name sounded familiar but he couldn't bring to mind who they were or what they'd done. And out here he had no way to contact Mr Bellington and ask for any information in the agency's files.

'A messenger came through several days ago with the news,' Father Flynn added. 'The gang robbed a bank in Santa Fe and a posse chased them out of New Mexico. I doubt they'll come this way, there's nothing for them here . . .'

'Not even in Northend?'

'No, not really. But it was something else I couldn't take a chance on. These children have been through enough without running the risk of coming up against hostile Apaches or murdering outlaws.'

Cobb almost smiled at the man's angry tone. 'When will they be here?'

'Should be tomorrow sometime.'

'The nuns aren't travelling on their own, are they?'

'Oh no. They're with a wagon driver and a guard. Both experienced men who won't take any risks. They'll travel as quickly as they can because Sister Mary Joseph won't let them dawdle!'

That night after a supper of lamb stew, more stew than lamb, and apple pie with a hard-baked crust (Neil was the only one who wanted seconds of either), Cobb lay in bed, trying to sleep. The room was small with plain whitewashed walls and a bed so tiny he was scared that if he rolled over he'd fall out. Both mattress and pillow were rock-hard and the sheet scratchy.

But it wasn't the discomfort keeping him awake; he'd slept in much worse places. No, he was still worried about the responsibility of looking after nuns and children when Apaches and outlaws might cause trouble. He thought he would be a match for the Indians and outlaws, he wasn't so sure about the nuns and the orphans!

THREE

'Are the children ready?' Sister Mary Joseph asked.

She looked across to where the five Mexican children – three boys and two girls – sat around the remains of the camp-fire, quietly finishing their breakfast.

'Almost, Sister,' Sister Catherine replied. 'Will we be at the mission today?' Trying not to sigh, she stared at the empty, grey-green expanse of desert leading towards the mauve line of distant foothills.

'I hope so. Early this afternoon I should think. We only have to cross those hills and the trail is fairly straightforward.'

'Thank goodness,' Catherine murmured.

Thank goodness indeed, Mary Joseph gave her own sigh of relief. This hadn't exactly been an easy journey. The children were all right. Mary Joseph behaved as she usually did with children and ignored them as much as possible. The guard and the wagon driver, both young Mexicans, were all right. She'd made similar journeys with them before and they knew what to do and when to do it.

No, much as she didn't like to admit it, her fellow nun was the problem.

Sister Catherine was young, only nineteen, pretty and lively. And although she tried hard to be dedicated she was finding the confines of the nunnery a bit too confining and wanted some excitement and adventure before taking her final vows. She also loved children and had volunteered, no, *begged*, to come along. Thinking it would help her find her faith, Mother Superior had agreed.

Mary Joseph had expressed doubts. She had always been accompanied by a nun as experienced as she, both in looking after children, who were not always as grateful at having their lives rearranged as others thought they should be, and in desert travel, which could be demanding and dangerous. But Mother Superior had reminded her of her vows, one of which was obedience. With misgivings Mary Joseph had obeyed.

They had hardly left the convent and started along the trail than Sister Catherine obviously had her own doubts. Although she didn't say anything, certainly didn't complain, it was clear she found the journey tough and hated the heat, the dust and the monotony of sitting in the back of an uncomfortable, slow-moving wagon.

Still, she was good with the children and Mary Joseph could leave their care to her.

'And will the Bellington's detective be at the mission waiting for us?' Catherine asked.

'He should be,' Mary Joseph said sourly.

Because that was the worst thing of all. That Father Flynn, of all people, should think she might need help and had gone about securing that help without first consulting her. She had done the journey several times before and had never had need of help. She could cope now.

Oh, she had been told his reasons: Indians and outlaws. Or rather rumours about them. Mary Joseph hadn't reached her forty-third year by being scared of rumours.

'I've never met a private detective before,' Catherine went on. 'I was surprised when you told me about him. I wonder what he'll be like.'

'Goodness knows. A nuisance I expect. I just hope he doesn't get in my way.'

Catherine looked shocked and her pale skin flushed. 'Oh, Sister, how can you speak so uncharitably? He's only here doing his job. And supposing something does go wrong? We might need his help for the good of the children. You should think of them. How awful would you feel if anything happened to hurt them?'

To prevent herself saying something uncharitable to the girl, Mary Joseph gritted her teeth together. It wasn't the first time Catherine had spoken naïvely or persisted in seeing the other side of an argument. Mary Joseph might be a nun, had never wanted to be anything else, but she was also realistic enough to know that while such turning of the other cheek might be what nuns should strive to achieve it wasn't always natural; or possible. Especially on the frontier.

Not the most sympathetic or patient of people, she tried to make allowances, told herself that Catherine was only young and would soon learn. But she was also quite sure she herself had never been that innocent. Or good. And she certainly hoped she had never been that damn annoying!

'Please, Sister, we are ready to leave,' the wagon driver came up to them, hat respectfully in hand. He was anxious to get under way before it became too hot.

Mary Joseph nodded in agreement. 'Sister Catherine, please see the children into the wagon.'

She glanced across at them. Black hair, dark eyes and dark skin, unmistakably Mexican despite their English style store-bought clothes.

Mary Joseph didn't particularly like children, and most children were scared of her, but she always did her best for those in her charge. She was impressed by their bravery and felt sorry for them. Young, orphaned usually in violent circumstances, left alone in the world. These were the lucky ones, going on to families, who would look after them and, she hoped, love them; and God help them if Mary Joseph found out otherwise.

Some were too tormented or too resentful of their misfortunes to make what Mother Superior called 'good and grateful children' but these five had posed no problems.

Thanks mainly to the brother and sister, Ernesto

and Isabella. Ernesto was ten, his sister a year younger. When their parents were killed in a runaway wagon accident, they had buried the bodies and walked for miles into the nearest town to tell the authorities. With no near relatives they had been sent to the nunnery and from the very beginning were thankful for all that was done for them, determined to make the best of an awful situation.

Mary Joseph had fought Mother Superior tooth and nail in her determination that the brother and sister wouldn't be separated but would go to the same family. Luckily a family willing to have two orphans had been found.

On the journey the two youngsters had decided to take charge and look after the other three: Manuel and Jaime who were seven and Maria six, all of whose parents had been killed in various Apache raids. They had persuaded the three younger children, who weren't quite so certain, that they should be happy that white families wanted to help them and should look forward to their new lives. It wouldn't be like living with their own parents but nothing could change what had happened and it was better than being in an orphanage. It was a chance and they should take it.

'Come along, children.' Clapping her hands Catherine hurried over to where they waited. 'Into the wagon. We'll reach the mission today, won't you like that? You'll see Father Flynn and then we'll go on to Northend and your new homes. We're all ready, Sister.'

'Good.' Mary Joseph climbed into the wagon, trying not to be annoyed at the girl's trilling tones.

The guard sat up front and the driver, after making sure nothing was left behind, joined him. He clicked the horses forward into a steady walk and the wagon lumbered on its way, leaving behind a small rise of dust.

Mary Joseph looked at her charges, receiving polite smiles from Ernesto and Isabella, while the other three ducked their heads and refused to look at her. As usual, little Maria clutched an old rag-doll to her chest. She had saved it from her burnt-out home and wouldn't go anywhere without it. Mother Superior said it was childish and should be taken from her. But Mary Joseph could see no harm in it and not for the first time overruled Mother Superior.

'We'll soon be there,' Catherine sang out. 'The Mission of San Francisco! It sounds so romantic.'

They had been travelling for almost an hour, had reached the edge of the foothills, when the attack came.

FOUR

'Do you think it'll be comfortable enough for Ernesto and Isabella?' Linda Pruitt stood back and surveyed the small room with its two low beds divided by a home-made chest of drawers, rag rug on the floor and hooks for clothes on the wall behind the door.

'I'm sure it will, Ma,' Gavin said. His mother had even managed to find a couple of colourful vases to place on the windowsill.

He put an arm around her shoulders. He knew how sad she felt because this had once been the bedroom of her two little daughters, who'd died almost three years ago in a smallpox epidemic sweeping this part of the country.

'You will find out from Mayor Drummond when they'll be here, won't you?'

'Yeah, Ma. Don't worry.' He gave her a squeeze. 'Everything will be fine, you'll see.'

'I do hope so,' his mother said. 'They've been through so much, I want them to be happy here.'

'I bet they will.' Gavin glanced out of the window

26

at the sky where dawn was streaking the clouds with pink. 'I'll have to be on my way now.'

'Gavin, you will be careful, won't you?'

'Yeah,' Gavin promised, with a little sigh. He loved his mother but since the death of her daughters she had worried so much about him, treated him like a young boy, that there were times he felt smothered. He hoped that with the arrival of the Mexican orphans she would worry about them instead.

'You know what your father wants, don't you?'

'Yeah, nails and baling wire.'

'And perhaps you could buy Isabella some ribbons for her hair and something for Ernesto. What? Maybe some liquorice sticks. He's sure to like them. That is if you have money enough.'

And something for his mother, Gavin decided, something to cheer the lonely life she led.

He let himself out of the farmhouse. His father was already at work over by the barn. He looked up and gave his son a wave but that was all, he was too busy to come over and speak to him for there was always so much to do.

Built of adobe, the farmhouse perched at the edge of a creek. This long into the year, the creek was almost dry, just a sliver of water running along the middle, the rest sand and dust. And the farm itself, dependent on water, was a poor dirt affair, needing constant work. Weeds grew faster than the vegetables, the vegetables had to be watered each day, the livestock had to be fed and watered. Walls needed building or repairing.

It was a hard life and a hard land: scrub, sage-brush and creosote bushes, accompanied by the sun burning out of a sky of metal-blue. Little rain, especially in the summer months.

And not for the first time Gavin wondered why anyone thought the Homestead Act could succeed out here or how his father could have been deceived into believing a prosperous farm could be built out of 160 acres of desert. But Eric Pruitt had been tired of labouring on someone else's farm for little in the way of wages, finding it difficult to provide for his growing family and so, not listening to advice or his wife's objections, he had allowed himself to be deceived.

They had come out here five years ago, when Gavin was fourteen, knowing nothing about Arizona or how to farm its soil. Their early optimism of a better life had soon faded away. They had almost given up several times in the first couple of years, especially when there wasn't enough to eat. But where would they have gone, what would they have done? As Pruitt said they had no choice but to stick it out; things would surely get better.

And things had. While the farm might never be called prosperous there was usually enough produce to sell in Northend once a month. Today, the back of the buckboard was full of vegetables and the fruit pies his mother spent hours baking.

As he drove the buckboard towards the gate opening on to the rough desert trail, Gavin had to pass the lonely graves of his two sisters. He never saw the wooden crosses and the pile of rocks so that animals wouldn't scavenge, without missing the little girls, although otherwise he was usually too busy to give them much thought.

Gavin could hardly wait for the arrival of the two Mexican children. He would then have help with the farmwork and his mother would have help in the home. They would both have company. He was still amazed that his mother, missing her daughters so much, had agreed to foster them.

Northend's mayor, Paul Drummond, had called just over a month ago, suggesting they might like to take in two orphans. At first Linda Pruitt had refused but she was persuaded when Drummond pointed out that helping two orphaned Mexican children would be in no way disloyal to her dead daughters and there was no question of them taking the little girls' places. The fact that Father Flynn, who ran the mission, was involved had helped her to make up her mind. And now she looked forward to their coming, wanted to love them.

Three other children were coming to Northend. One, a girl, going to the childless couple who owned the café, a boy on to Everly's farm and the third to the owner of the livery stable, who, getting on in years and suffering from arthritis, needed help with saddling and bridling the horses. Their arrival would make a difference to so many people and Gavin just hoped nothing went wrong. He would hate to see his mother's hopes dashed.

Gavin enjoyed his monthly journey into

Northend. The length of the drive meant he had to stay in town overnight. Not that the town had a great deal to see and do but the farm was lonely and at least here were buildings and people.

Northend existed mostly for the ranchers, and a few farmers, in the outlying district. Several silver-mines were also located in the nearby hills and the miners occasionally came down to have their silver assayed. Thus it was usually quite lively, with a small but thriving redlight district, which Gavin intended to visit as soon as he could.

The town's few stores, café and tiny hotel were situated round the main plaza, in the middle of which was a deep well, without whose water Northend would cease to exist. Not many people were about when he arrived, most taking a siesta during the hottest hours of the day but the stores remained open and a couple of horses were tied to the railings outside them.

He sold the vegetables in the general store and the pies to the café owner, getting fair prices for everything. And left the buckboard and horse at the livery. Before doing anything else he decided to visit the mayor to find out the news.

Paul Drummond was the owner or, as he deemed it, the chairman of the real-estate office. As such he always wore store-bought clothes and shoes. He came from New York and thought he knew better than anyone else. In his forties, he was full of more importance than being mayor of a small town like Northend warranted. As far as Gavin was aware it was more a case of no one else wanting the position, although it would have hurt Drummond's feelings to tell him so. While most people sniggered about him behind his back they did, on the whole, respect him to his face and were in awe of his Eastern education.

The office was situated on the corner of the short street leading to the church. When Gavin went inside, Drummond had a map of the county spread out on his desk and was marking it with different coloured blobs. Probably starting up one of his grand schemes for selling plots of land which so far hadn't amounted to much.

'Hallo, Mr Drummond.' Gavin sank into the chair before the desk. 'Hot out there today.'

'Sure is.' Although Drummond's office was cool enough with its thick adobe walls and small windows. 'What can I do for you? Is it about the orphans?'

'Yeah. I wondered if you knew when they were likely to arrive?'

Drummond leant forward on his desk and smiled with self-satisfaction. 'They're on their way! Should be here in a few days' time. Isn't that good news?' He gave Gavin no chance to reply but hurried on, 'I've asked Father Flynn that when they set out from the mission he sends a messenger on here so I can tell everyone. Then I intend we should hold a grand reception so the children are welcomed properly to their new homes in Northend!'

Gavin hid both a smile and a sigh. Drummond sounded as if he was talking about important dignitaries, not five orphaned children. Children who would probably be apprehensive about what was going to happen to them and where they were going to go, perhaps scared, and who might prefer not to have a fuss made. Gavin didn't say anything. Drummond was unlikely to take any notice of him. And he was doing what he considered best, although he probably hoped he would gain recognition of his part in their arrival.

'I'll tell Ma and Pa. They'll be pleased.'

'As will everyone involved. I can't tell you how pleased *I am* at how this has turned out. Perhaps I can arrange for more children to come here.'

Gavin decided to leave before he had to suffer one of Drummond's lengthy speeches. At the door he stopped and said, 'By the way, has there been any more news of that outlaw band said to be heading this way? Any sign?'

He sounded worried. The Pruitt farm was isolated and although it had never been attacked, by either Indian or outlaw, it was a constant threat.

Drummond shook his head. 'No, nothing more. It's unlikely they'll come to Northend. We haven't got a bank for the bastards to rob.'

'We ain't got much in the way of law either.'

Drummond frowned. 'I know that.'

The last marshal had deserted some time in the spring to work a friend's silver-mine and they were left with Les Smith, the town constable, who was fifty, fat and incompetent.

'I've raised the subject more than once at meetings of the town council. Unsuccessfully. All the while it's quiet they don't want to spend money on something they think unnecessary.'

Made the excuse that what good lawman would want to come here and if one did they risked losing him to the mines.

'What'll happen if one day it isn't quiet?'

'Then I guess, Gavin, they'll be sorry and it'll be too late.'

Gavin shrugged; it wasn't his problem. He stepped out into the noonday heat, shutting the door behind him and promptly forgot all about the orphans, the outlaws and Drummond's self-importance. The rest of the day was his.

He would get a bath and a haircut, his fair hair was decidedly tangled, and head for the saloons.

Have a drink and find out if Cindy was free. His mother wouldn't approve of Cindy but there were things his mother never needed to learn.

FIVE

The attack came out of nowhere. One minute it was quiet. The next, sunlight flashed along a gun barrel, followed at once by a loud boom and the guard's chest exploded in a bloody spray. Without even uttering a cry he tumbled off the buckboard to land in the dust.

Sister Catherine's scream was echoed by the screams of the children. Quickly Ernesto knocked his sister to the bottom of the wagon and threw himself on top of Maria.

The driver hauled on the reins of the startled horses to stop them bolting. It was a mistake. Maybe if the animals had been allowed to run they might have escaped. Maybe. As it was by the time Mary Joseph gathered her senses and yelled, 'Drive!' six horsemen had thundered out of the rocks where they'd been hiding, galloping towards them.

Mary Joseph turned to Catherine. The girl was cowering down, holding her hands together as if in prayer. 'Get the children out!' As Catherine hesitated she gave her a push. 'Hurry.'

34

'What do they want?'

'I don't know. See to the children. Go on! Now!' Mary Joseph swung back to the driver. 'No!' she cried as she saw he had grabbed up the guard's rifle.

She was too late. Another shot. And the driver was flung back into the wagon, landing at her feet. Mary Joseph paused. Then knowing she could do nothing for him, that the children were her main concern, she jumped down to the ground. And glanced round.

'This way.' She pointed to a jumble of boulders a short distance away.

'We'll never make it,' Catherine sobbed. 'We're going to be killed.' Her voice rose hysterically.

Mary Joseph ignored her. The riders were almost upon them. Their position was hopeless but she couldn't just stand here and not at least try to escape.

'Ernesto, look after Isabella.' Immediately the boy caught hold of his sister's hand and they raced away. 'Sister Catherine, take the boys. Come here, Maria.' She picked the terrified girl up into her arms and began to run.

Who were the men? What did they intend to do? The frightened thoughts spun through Mary Joseph's mind. What did they want? To rob them? If so, they'd be unlucky. They had nothing worth stealing. Or did they have something more sinister in mind? She hoped they weren't going to be killed out here in the desert but she was fearful Sister Catherine was right and that would be their fate, that no one would ever discover what had happened.

And where, oh where, was Mr Bellington's private detective when she needed him? Why wasn't he here instead of taking his ease with Father Flynn at the mission?

They almost made it to the boulders, although what she would have done if they had Mary Joseph didn't know. But then, suddenly, the riders were upon them, riding round them. She glimpsed wild faces, excited eyes – white men, not Apaches, which maybe was a relief – and horses looming above her, dust enveloping everything.

She put Maria down and gathered the children to her. None of them was crying, which was more than could be said for Sister Catherine, who stood, hands over her eyes, wailing in terror. But all five looked petrified and Mary Joseph lost her own fear in her anger. The children had been through so much and now here were these bastards frightening them, threatening them, all over again. Even worse, she could do nothing to stop them.

'Grab the kids!' one of the men yelled.

A horse was shoved forward and someone reached down, tugging Maria out of her grasp. The girl let out a panic-stricken howl.

'No!' Mary Joseph knocked at the man's arm. It did no good. Maria was torn roughly from her and flung over the man's saddle.

More hands caught at the other children.

'Stop it! Oh, please don't!' Catherine cried ineffectually.

Mary Joseph darted forward. With Catherine's cry of, 'Sister, don't!' in her ears, she clutched at the reins of the horse belonging to the man who seemed to be in charge. A young man, good-looking, she had time to note, with black, braided hair.

'Stop this!' she yelled.

For answer he laughed and pulled the horse away from her, forcing her to let go of the reins. With a vicious glint in his eyes he dug spurs into its sides, deliberately sending it leaping forward. Mary Joseph had no chance to move out of the way and it crashed into her. Losing her breath, she was knocked to the ground.

'Sister!' Along with the screams of the children, she heard Ernesto calling her name. Then blackness descended and she heard and saw no more.

As quickly as the outlaws had approached, they galloped away. Catherine ran a few steps after them, watching, then hurried back.

'Sister Mary Joseph, are you all right? Are you hurt?'

'There, I done told you how easy it'd be, didn't I?' Kenny Kelman bragged.

After their dash away from the scene of the ambush, the gang hadn't ridden very far before stopping for a while to rest and have something to eat and drink. Celebrate their victory. Why not? This time there was no pursuit.

'None of us hurt. No one coming after us. And because of them,' he nodded towards the children huddled together on the other side of the small camp-fire, 'a good profit at the end of it.'

Watching Kelman strut around, Worley grinned. Sometimes Kenny was just too full of himself but there was little doubt he usually came up with good ideas. Helping himself to another cup of coffee he said, 'What now?'

'Now? Someone rides for the mission. Tells Father Flynn we've got his precious kids and what we want for their safe return.'

'They will pay up, won't they?'

'Yeah. If they're so damn soft-hearted they're willing to take in a bunch of Mex kids, they'll pay to see they ain't hurt.'

Worley nodded. 'True.'

'Joe,' Kelman turned to the young man, 'you'd better go. You're our best rider.'

Joe nodded. 'OK, Kenny.'

'You know what to tell him, don't you? And where to meet us?'

'Yeah.' Joe went over to his horse and was soon galloping away.

'The rest of us will head for Northend. And you,' he turned towards Maria and shouted, 'stop that snivelling or I'll goddamn shut you up.'

Ernesto glared at the man and put an arm round the little girl, trying to comfort her.

'You ain't none of you got nothing to worry about,' Kelman went on, striding up and down in front of them. 'Your new folks will be glad to pay us for you and then you'll be let free to go to 'em.' This might have comforted the children had he not gone on, 'And if they don't then we'll take you back to Mexico and sell the lot of you to the mines.'

'Oh no,' Jaime sobbed. He knew all about the mines, for that had been where his father worked.

'Oh yeah. They always want kids to work deep down in the earth, real deep deep down where it's dark and scary and there ain't hardly no room. But you shouldn't worry 'bout that neither because the kids don't last long before they suffer and die.' With a huge guffaw Kelman turned away.

'He don't mean it,' Ernesto whispered to the others, thinking the man was so mean he probably did. He glanced at the rest of the gang. They were grinning. There would be no help from any of them.

'Oh, Ernesto, what are we going to do?' Isabella asked, with a little catch of fear in her voice.

'I don't think we can do anything.'

They weren't tied up, not even closely guarded, but they were being watched. And if they tried to run away, where could they go? Ernesto had no idea in which direction either mission or town was. And if they did somehow escape they would be little better off stuck in the desert, without water or horses, than kept here as prisoners, where hopefully they would be fed and where they would be let go as soon as the men got what they wanted.

And if they did try to get away, these men, with horses, would quickly catch up with them and punish them. Ernesto realized they were ruthless. Wouldn't hesitate to treat them badly.

'I'm scared,' Isabella said, tears welling in her eyes.

So was Ernesto.

'Hush. Don't worry,' he said, squeezing his sister's hand. 'Sister Mary Joseph won't let anything happen to us. She'll help us.'

But would she? The last Ernesto had seen of the nun, she was lying on the ground, hurt, unmoving. Supposing . . . supposing she was hurt badly, even killed?

SIX

'Sister!' Catherine cried. She reached her fellow nun and bent down by her, putting out a hand to touch her. 'Oh please say you're all right.'

Slowly Mary Joseph opened her eyes and sat up. Head spinning, she thought she was about to faint. But the feeling passed and thankfully she realized that, apart from an ache in her ribs where the horse had smashed into her, she hurt nowhere else.

'Sister, are you injured?'

'No, I don't think so.'

'Oh thank Heavens.'

'Help me up.' As Mary Joseph got to her feet, the ground seemed to lift beneath her but with an effort of will she ignored it. 'The children?'

'They've gone. Those awful men stole them.' A sob sounded in Catherine's voice. 'The poor mites. What will happen to them? And you could have been killed. That man banged his horse into you on purpose.'

'I know, but that doesn't matter. I'm not hurt. All that matters is the children.'

'Whatever shall we do?'

Mary Joseph gave a slight shake of her head.

'Who were they?'

'I imagine they were the outlaw gang we heard about.'

Catherine put a hand to her mouth. 'But why have they taken the children?'

'I don't know.' Mary Joseph could think of no reason for what had happened. But it was obvious the children had been stolen for a purpose and it meant that at least they were still alive. That they would remain safe was a hope to cling to.

'What shall we do?' Catherine repeated.

'First let's see how our driver is.'

Somewhat to Mary Joseph's annoyance, Catherine insisted on holding her arm to help her back to the wagon. She said nothing, knowing it was kindly meant but thinking that although her ribs hurt she wasn't an invalid.

The guard lay where he had fallen. Blood had seeped into the ground all round him.

'Is he dead?' Catherine whispered.

'Yes.' Mary Joseph ignored the girl's whimper of horror. She peered into the wagon. The driver lay motionless, huddled on his side, blood staining the left sleeve of his shirt. He wasn't dead but was clearly in no position to help them or even to drive the wagon.

'We should pray for them both.' Catherine reached for her rosary beads.

'There's no time for that.'

Catherine looked shocked. 'But, Sister, we must. Mother Superior would expect it.'

Mary Joseph took no notice. She knew Catherine thought her hard-hearted, unfeeling. But while she would mourn the guard, who had died just doing his job, been killed without being able to defend himself, that would have to be later, right now the living were her concern.

She climbed up beside the driver. As she turned him over he groaned and his eyes flickered briefly open but when she said, 'Don't worry. You're safe,' they closed again. He didn't wake again as quickly she tore his sleeve away. The bullet was still in his arm and the hole was still bleeding. All she could do was tie the sleeve tightly round the wound.

She turned to Catherine who was watching, wide-eyed. 'He needs to be gotten to the mission where Father Flynn can look after him.'

'What about the guard? Are we going to bury him?'

'No.' Where on earth did the girl get these ideas from? 'He'll have to be taken there as well. Given a proper burial. Help me lift his body into the back.'

'Oh, I'm not sure I can . . .' Catherine began.

Quailing under the other nun's stern and impatient look, she said no more but bit her lip. She caught hold of the guard's feet while Mary Joseph lifted his shoulders. He was a heavy man but somehow they managed to manoeuvre him on to the wagonbed.

'Here.' Mary Joseph passed Catherine a canteen of water.

She stared round at the empty desert. The tracks of the outlaws were clearly visible, for the moment. The fact that that might not last for long and then the outlaws' trail would become hard to follow, helped her make up her mind as to what she should do.

'Sister Catherine, are you able to drive the wagon?'

'Why yes. I was born in Texas.'

'Good. Then you can take it and these men on to the mission.'

'What do you mean? What are you going to do?'

'Someone must try and help the children.'

Slowly Catherine handed the canteen back to Mary Joseph and, as if she didn't understand what the nun was talking about, said, 'But they're gone!'

'And as we don't know how far the outlaws intend to take them or, more important, what their purpose is, then I must follow them and see where they go.'

There was a moment of quiet before Catherine let out a screech. 'You can't!'

'Yes, I can. And will.'

'They're on horseback. You'll never catch them up.'

'I can at least find out in which direction they're going.'

'But if the private detective is at the mission it'll be his job to do that.'

'I hope I'll be able to save him time in tracking them.' Time, Mary Joseph thought, was essential.

'The sooner we catch up with these bas. . . outlaws, the sooner the children will be rescued.'

'It could be dangerous.'

'I doubt it.'

'But if you're seen?'

'The men have long gone and they certainly won't be expecting anyone to be coming after them.'

Not so soon anyway.

'You can't go alone. I'm coming with you.' Catherine looked scared but determined.

'No.' Mary Joseph put a hand on her fellow nun's shoulder. 'The driver needs to be taken to the mission so his wound can be seen to. The guard needs to be buried. And Father Flynn must learn what's happened, as must the private detective.'

'Then please give up this idea and come with me,' Catherine begged.

'No, you must go alone,' Mary Joseph insisted and when Mary Joseph insisted on something very few people argued with her.

Catherine had been with her long enough to know when she'd made up her mind and nothing would change it. But she tried one more time by saying, 'I don't know the way.'

'It's easy now. Not far. All you have to do is drive up into the hills,' Mary Joseph pointed. 'Almost immediately you'll come to a stream. Turn right and follow it until you reach a valley. Once you do, you'll see the mission. You should be there within a couple of hours. Don't worry. You'll be all right and so will I.'

Catherine didn't look sure about that.

'You can then give the detective directions as to how to get back out here. And I'll leave him a trail to follow.'

'How?'

'By tearing pieces off the bottom of my habit and securing them under rocks. The black will show up against the grey and be easy to spot.'

'Your habit? Oh dear, Mother Superior won't like you doing that.'

'Mother Superior isn't here.' Mary Joseph made Catherine all the more shocked. 'Now, give me the full canteen of water and you can be on your way. We haven't got time to waste arguing.'

Knowing it was useless to say any more, Catherine climbed up on to the wagon seat and picked up the reins. 'I'll be as quick as I can,' she promised. 'Be careful.'

'Yes.' Mary Joseph nodded to the girl and stood watching as she drove away.

It was then she realized exactly what she'd done: she was all alone, in the desert, without a horse or a weapon. She almost raised a hand to call Catherine back. But she stopped herself. Mary Joseph rarely doubted her own abilities or the choices she made. She would manage. Anyway, if the private detective was worth his pay he would soon catch up.

And as the children had been in her care it was up to her to do her best for them. She would never be able to forgive herself if anything happened to them when she could have prevented it.

With a little sigh and a little prayer she slung the canteen over her shoulder, lifted the skirt of her habit and turned round.

As she did so, something laying on the ground caught her eye. She stopped. It was Maria's rag doll. The poor child. She must have dropped it and now would be missing it so much, crying for it. Giving in to a spurt of anger at what had happened, she picked up the doll and carefully put it into her pocket. She would give it back to the little girl when she rescued her.

SEVEN

'Shouldn't they be here by now?' Cobb said. Already the afternoon shadows were lengthening into evening.

Even Father Flynn was starting to look worried. 'Well, I was expecting them earlier but I suppose desert travel being what it is something could have happened to delay them.'

'Perhaps I'd better ride out, try to find them.'

'Mr Cobb!' They were interrupted by Neil's shout. He was in the bell tower, watching what passed for a trail coming from California. 'I can see them.'

Cobb and Father Flynn hurried to join Neil at the top of the tower. A wagon had emerged from the slope of the hills and was making its way across the valley, leaving a high trail of dust in its wake.

Father Flynn stared at it and then looked at Cobb. With some dismay in his voice, he said, 'But where are the children?'

By the time the three men raced outside the

wagon had drawn closer. It was obvious it had been driven fast for some while – the two horses were speckled with foamy sweat – and by a nun.

'Oh hell!' Father Flynn said, quite shocking both Cobb and Neil. 'What the hell has happened?'

The wagon was pulled to a halt in front of them. Before Cobb could reach her, Sister Catherine had half-jumped, half-fallen off the seat.

She cried out, 'Father! Oh, Father, the children have been snatched!' and collapsed on the ground.

Immediately Father Flynn took charge. He picked the nun up and ordered Cobb and Neil to carry the wounded man into the infirmary. Other workers appeared to take the dead man into the church.

'Is she hurt?' Cobb said as Father Flynn laid Catherine on one of the beds.

'It doesn't look like it. I think she's just fainted from the heat and exertion.'

'I wonder what she meant?'

'You can ask once I've treated her. Perhaps you'd leave me. I might have to remove Sister Catherine's habit and it wouldn't be right for you to see her in a state of undress.'

'Of course, I understand. Is there anything Neil and I can do?'

'A grave will have to be dug for the dead man. Will you do that?'

'Yes.'

'Good. Once I've seen to these two I'll say a mass for him and he can then be buried.' Speed was of the essence in the desert heat.

Cobb went to find Neil and led the way out to the cemetery, situated behind the church.

Digging the grave was hard, hot work and they didn't have the chance to speak to one another. But all the time Cobb was thinking and worrying. Why had the children – Mexican orphans - been snatched? Or was Sister Catherine wrong? And where was Sister Mary Joseph?

An hour or so later, Cobb and Neil sat in the main room waiting for Father Flynn. When he came in, Cobb said, 'Are the sister and the driver all right?'

'Yes, thank God. The driver lost quite a lot of blood but the wound wasn't bad once I got the bullet out.' Father Flynn was obviously a man of many talents. 'And as I hoped there's nothing wrong with Sister Catherine that a little rest won't cure.' He sank down on the bench and accepted the glass of water Neil poured for him. 'And she has managed to tell me a little more of her story.'

Quickly he told them about the attack and its aftermath.

'Sister Mary Joseph has remained in the desert?' Cobb was incredulous. 'What the hell does she think she's doing?'

But Father Flynn, whilst also appreciating how foolish were the nun's actions, couldn't resist smiling. 'I'm not surprised. Sister Mary Joseph doesn't particularly like children but she will fight tooth and nail for those in her charge. This is just like her.'

'That's all very well.' Cobb hadn't liked some of his clients but he'd have been prepared to lay down his life to defend and protect them. 'But what good does she think she can do? Doesn't she realize the danger she might be in?' Not so much from the outlaws, who had probably long gone, but from the harsh, unforgiving land.

'Sister Mary Joseph will put her trust in her faith,' Father Flynn said simply. 'And do what she believes to be right.'

Cobb sighed grumpily. Sister Mary Joseph sounded a wilful and stubborn handful.

'Mr Cobb, do you think it's this Kelman gang who's responsible?'

'I imagine so.' Unless there were two outlaw bands in the area, which didn't seem very likely.

'What are you going to do?'

'Go after them. As soon as possible.'

Father Flynn nodded. 'What will you need?'

'Some supplies. Food. Water. Horses for me and Neil. And the wagon and fresh horses. Is there someone here who can drive it?'

Father Flynn paused to consider and into the silence a girl's voice said, 'I can drive for you.'

They all turned to see Sister Catherine standing in the doorway. Neil gaped open-mouthed. He had no idea what nuns were like but even in her shapeless black habit and wimple framing her face, he thought she looked too young to be one and much too pretty, with pale skin, full mouth and large brown eyes.

'Sister Catherine!' Father Flynn exclaimed, standing up and going over to her. 'You shouldn't be up. You should be resting.'

'No, I'm fine.' Catherine allowed herself to be led to the table. She sat opposite Cobb. 'I want to help.'

'I'm not sure that's a good idea,' Cobb began, thinking one nun was already out in the desert and he didn't want to be responsible for another one, especially one who might delay them.

'Please.' Tears came into the girl's eyes. 'I can't just wait here. I'm so worried about Sister Mary Joseph and those poor children. I was meant to be caring for them but I was too scared and concerned with my own safety to do anything to stop them being taken.'

'What could you have done?' Father Flynn patted her hand. 'You might have been hurt if you'd tried.'

'I know that in my head but my heart tells me differently. Please, Mr Cobb, you must let me help. Besides, I can lead you straight back to where the attack took place.'

Cobb hesitated. He didn't think it would be any too difficult to find the spot; all he had to do was follow the wagon tracks. And he really didn't want Sister Catherine along. At the same time she looked so desperate he was afraid she might do something as silly as her fellow nun.

So when she said, 'You might need my help with the children,' which was quite true, he nodded. 'All right.'

'Oh, thank you!' she cried. 'When are we going?'

'As soon as possible.'

'The sister really should rest,' Father Flynn objected.

'We can't wait. There's still a couple of hours' daylight left. We can use 'em.'

'Mr Cobb is right, Father. I can manage, really.'

'I'll go and start getting together what we need,' Neil offered.

'OK.' Once Neil had gone, Cobb turned to Catherine, who sat twisting her hands in her lap. 'How many men were there?'

'Six, I think.'

'Did you see what they looked like?'

'No.' The girl shook her head. 'I'm sorry. They weren't wearing masks or anything like that but it all happened so fast and I was so frightened.'

'Don't worry. It doesn't matter.' Cobb paused then said, 'Did they say anything about why they were taking the children? What they intended to do?'

Again Catherine shook her head. 'They didn't say a word.'

An hour later Father Flynn waved the three of them goodbye. Sister Catherine drove the wagon, Cobb and Neil riding on either side and slightly ahead. He waited, watching until they were almost out of sight. He was very worried. Not just over the children and Sister Mary Joseph but over allowing Sister Catherine to go along with Cobb. Mary Joseph was a law unto herself, probably wouldn't have taken any notice of whatever he, or anyone else, told her, but he should have refused to let Catherine go. She was little more than a child herself. Supposing something happened to her? Or happened to any of them.

He couldn't believe any of this. Those poor children. He thought he was doing right in bringing them to Northend. They had suffered so much violence, lost their families in tragic circumstances and deserved a new, safe life. Instead they had been seized by violent outlaws. It wasn't fair. If only he'd sent Cobb out to meet the wagon rather than keeping him here . . . but although he'd taken the precaution of sending for a private detective, in his heart he hadn't really expected the wagon and its occupants to be in danger. How wrong could he be?

Shaking his head he went into the church to pray for the safety of all those involved and for the swift return of the children. He would also have to prepare the mass for the dead guard, who lay on a wooden bier near to the altar.

With its small high windows and thick doors and walls, the church struck cool and dim, especially to someone coming from the relentless sunshine outside. Father Flynn never entered it without a feeling of peace coming over him, but this time, almost immediately, he was aware of another presence. Someone else was in the church. Skulking behind one of the pillars. Up to no good.

He came to a halt, heart thudding with sudden fright. 'Who's there? Come on out!'

A stranger stepped into the aisle. He was young and tall, dressed roughly, with long hair and a thick black moustache. His hand hovered above the revolver in its worn holster.

Instinctively Father Flynn knew this was one of

the bandits who had attacked the wagon, a member of the Kelman gang. Who else would be here smirking at him? Fright gave way to fury.

'What do you want?' he demanded. 'This is God's house. A place of peace not guns.'

The man grinned. 'Hey now, no need to be like that. Got a message for you, is all. You want it or not?'

The priest swallowed his anger. Of course he wanted the message. He nodded.

'We want paying for the Mex kids.'

Father Flynn almost laughed. 'Then you've come to the wrong place.'

'Oh, not from you, old man, we know the mission ain't got no money.'

Father Flynn wondered how, although it was probably no great secret.

'But I guess them real good folks in Northend will be glad to pay up. Don't you? Say a hundred dollars for each kid. That ain' t so very much.'

Altogether that amounted to $500. It sounded a great deal to Father Flynn. And he wondered how it would sound to the people in Northend, who, on the whole, weren't well off.

'I don't know if they can afford it.'

'They'd goddamn better. We'll be waiting at Wheeler's Canyon. Know where that is?'

'Yes.'

A bleak, empty spot, surrounded by cliffs.

'Good. You got two days. No longer. If someone don't come with our money by then the kids'll be killed.' As he spoke the man ran a finger across his throat in a cutting motion.

'How dare you!' Father Flynn stepped forward.

'Now, now. None of that.' The man wagged his finger. 'Oh, by the way, only one person is to deliver the money. He's to be unarmed. Anything else the kids'll die. Understand? Any law and—'

'Yes I know. The kids will be killed,' Father Flynn interrupted, red-faced with fury.

'You got it, old man! Now, as there ain't much time you'd better get on with it, hadn't you? Be seeing you.'

And with that the young man sauntered out of the church leaving Father Flynn staring impotently after him.

EIGHT

It was easy to see where the attack had taken place. Not only was the blood from the guard's body still visible but all around the ground was scuffed up by several horses.

'We tried to make it to those boulders.' Catherine pointed. 'We didn't succeed.' She wiped her eyes and lowered them to look at the ground.

Cobb said, 'What could you have done if you'd reached them? There were six armed outlaws against just you and Sister Mary Joseph.'

Mention of the other nun made him look round. He'd hoped she would have realized the futility of staying out here alone, following the outlaws, and instead waited for rescue. But he saw no sign of her.

'Which way did they go?'

'That way.' Catherine indicated the north.

'Are you sure?' Cobb was surprised. 'Not towards Mexico?' Which seemed the sensible choice.

'No. That way. Of course they might have changed direction once in the foothills.'

'Yeah, they might if they thought to deceive anyone coming in pursuit,' Cobb agreed, thinking it unlikely they would bother. But why weren't the gang taking Mexican orphans back to Mexico? Where were they going?

He looked round. The sun was sinking below the hills to the west. He was worried about Sister Catherine, who looked tired, worn out by her experiences. And it would soon be dark, and cold. Almost time to stop for the night. But not here, where there was no shelter. The hills were nearby and there they would also find wood to make a fire.

'We'll stop soon,' he promised. 'Rest up for the night.'

Sister Mary Joseph paused to tear a piece of material from the already torn and dusty bottom of her habit. She bent to place it carefully under a rock so it wouldn't be disturbed. As she stood up she stretched, trying to ease the kinks out of her back, which was aching after the long and difficult climb. At least she had on stout shoes or else her feet would already be cut and bruised.

She shivered, knowing she would soon have to stop for the night. The shadows were deepening, were almost impenetrable near the edge of the hills and the wind was picking up, making it cooler. She would suffer an uncomfortable night, with no shelter, nothing to eat, no way to make a fire and only water to drink.

What had possessed her to do such a foolish

thing? She could never hope to catch up with the outlaws and the children. In places their trail was already becoming hard to follow . . . and that was the point. To anyone coming on behind it would be harder still, take longer to follow, even for an experienced tracker. And the longer the children were with the men, the more perilous their situation and the more difficult it would become to rescue them.

Mary Joseph looked back down the long slope of the hill. The hope that someone might be on their way to help her died. No one and nothing moved out there. Yet surely Catherine must have long since reached the mission, it couldn't have taken her that long, and surely, oh surely, help was on its way. The private detective wouldn't delay until the morning, would he? She'd certainly have something to say to him if so!

With no one around to notice, Mary Joseph gave in to exhaustion and, she had to admit, only to herself, fear. She slumped on the ground, resting her back against a rock. Really she was getting much too old for this sort of reckless behaviour, would ache all over tomorrow. Telling herself off for giving in to self-pity she took a long sip of water, crossed her arms in front of her and prepared to go to sleep.

It was late when the sixth outlaw, Joe, returned to the camp the others had made in the rocks. The rest gathered round him, listening intently.

'Can you hear what they're saying?' Isabella whispered.

'No.' Ernesto shook his head. 'But look, they're

happy enough.' The men were laughing and joking. Perhaps that was a good sign. If they were happy they were unlikely to get angry and take their anger out on the children. 'You must sleep now, like them.' He glanced at Manuel, Jaime and Maria who were all cuddled up together, sleeping restlessly, worn out after the hard ride to get here. 'We might have another long journey tomorrow.'

'I'm still hungry.'

They had been given water and some biscuits, not much between them but at least they weren't going to be starved. Ernesto didn't think they would be given any more even if he dared ask. Which he didn't.

'You must be strong,' he told his sister. 'Help me look after the others. Like you helped me when our parents died. I can't do it all by myself. Please.'

Isabella thought for a moment then nodded. 'I'll try.'

'Hush,' Ernesto warned as the man called Kenny, the leader of the gang, glared across at them. Kenny was a bad man, might punish them if they didn't do what he ordered and he'd ordered them to go to sleep.

He lay down, trying to get comfortable on the ground. He put his arms around Isabella and soon her eyes closed and she drifted into sleep. Ernesto stayed awake longer, worried over how he was responsible for them all. But he knew Sister Mary Joseph would expect him to do his best and not give up. He didn't want to disappoint her.

*

'This is goin' well,' Kelman said, grinning across at Brad Worley. 'We'll soon have money again.'

'Not much though,' Worley pointed out, perhaps the only person able to criticize Kelman without running the risk of getting shot. 'Not as much as from a bank robbery.'

'Ain't no banks out here,' Kelman pointed out. 'It'll be enough for us to ride into Mexico and spend a while enjoying ourselves in the cantinas and brothels.'

That made Worley's eyes light up. They often ran to Mexico and knew several places where they would receive a warm welcome from the *señoritas*.

'Anyway, if all goes right I've gotta idea about how we maybe can get more.' Kelman grinned again, obviously having something in mind but not prepared to share it for the moment. He wanted to keep quiet in case it wasn't possible and to make himself look even better if it was. 'Once it's safe to cross back from Mexico we can recruit a couple more men, go into California. No one'll expect us there and we should find some easy pickings.'

Worley nodded. Like Kelman, he couldn't see how anything could go wrong.

It didn't take Cobb and the others long to reach the hills. So far the trail had been easy to follow but once they climbed amongst the rocks and scrub it started to peter out. Cobb didn't know what he would do if the trail vanished. . . .

'Mr Cobb!' Neil's cry interrupted his gloomy thoughts. 'Over here.'

Both men dismounted and Neil pointed to a large piece of black cloth secured under a rock. Cobb nodded with satisfaction. Mary Joseph was acting sensibly. She hadn't wasted time, or her habit, all the while the trail was obvious and she had made sure the cloth stayed put.

'Is it hers?' Catherine called from her perch on the wagon seat.

'Yeah.'

'Oh, thank goodness.'

Cobb stared along the way they would have to go. Rocks and undergrowth encroached on either side and he thought it might prove hard going, especially for a wagon.

He turned to Neil and said, 'Maybe tomorrow it'd be best if you drove the wagon. Sister Catherine can either ride in the back or ride your horse.'

She was able to handle the wagon but she wasn't very strong and he didn't want any accidents slowing them down.

'OK,' Neil agreed. 'Do you know where we are or where we're headed?'

'No. I wish I did but I've never been in this area before.'

'Me either.'

'We can stop here for the night,' Cobb decided after a quick look round. 'It's as good a place as any.'

There was plenty of room and scrub and twigs for a fire while high rocks would hide the flames from prying eyes. He went back to where Catherine waited and helped her to the ground.

'I'll see to the horses,' she offered.

'No, Sister, you sit down. Rest.'

'Please, there's no need to consider me.'

'Don't worry, Neil will look after the animals and start a fire, won't you?'

'Yes, sir.' Uncomfortable in the presence of the pretty nun, not knowing what to say to her or how to act, Neil was only glad to have something to do.

'Do you think we'll catch up with the children soon?' Catherine asked as she collapsed on the ground, rubbing her arms.

'I hope so. Early start tomorrow. So once we've had something to eat, get some sleep, both of you.'

NINE

'Must you go?' Cindy asked.

Gavin paused in doing up his shirt to look at the naked girl lying in the bed. He grinned. He always sought Cindy out when he came to town. They hadn't slept much last night.

'Yeah. Pity. But I've got a lot of supplies to buy and Pa is waiting for them.'

'You will come back soon, won't you?' And with a mischievous smile the girl sat up in bed, revealing her small breasts.

'You can bet on that!'

Gavin let himself out of Cindy's room and went downstairs to where the saloon was being opened up to start the day. The bartender was sweeping the floor and he smiled as Gavin went by him. Feeling pleased with himself and with life in general, the young man grinned back. Being a farmer out here might be unrewarding most of the time but it certainly had its good moments.

When he arrived, the plaza was also coming

awake. A couple of the stores were already open for business and a few women had gathered by the well, not to collect water but to gossip before the heat of the day drove them indoors. It wouldn't take him long to buy what he needed and then he could start back for the farm.

Suddenly the morning quiet was broken by the sound of pounding hoofs. A rider came into view. He pulled his tired, sweating horse to a stop in front of the real-estate office, which was open. Mayor Drummond kept long hours not because he had a successful business but more likely, some said unkindly, because he wanted to stay out of his wife's way.

The rider was a young Mexican and Gavin thought he recognized him, wondering where he could have seen him before. Then, with a jolt, remembering. He was a worker at Father Flynn's mission.

His heart lifted. The rider must have come with a message that the children were on their way. But then his heart sank; if it was simply that why would the rider be in such a hurry he'd risked killing his horse?

Was something wrong? Gavin broke into a run, crossing the plaza to the office. When he went inside he knew his fears were confirmed. Mayor Drummond was on his feet, white-faced beneath his sun-tan, leaning forward on hands clenched on the desktop.

'What is it? What's happening?'

Drummond turned from the messenger to look at

the young man. In a disbelieving voice he said, 'It's the children. They've been kidnapped and are being held for ransom!'

'What!' Gavin was stunned by the news.

'It's true, *señor*,' the Mexican said with a little nod. 'A bad man came to Father Flynn yesterday evening. Father already knew something was wrong because the guard with the wagon was killed and the driver shot.'

'What about the nuns?'

'They are safe, *señor*.'

'The bastards are demanding five hundred dollars,' Drummond explained. 'Or they're threatening to kill the children.'

'Oh my God.' Gavin could hardly believe what he was hearing. 'They wouldn't do that, would they?'

'It is what bad man say, *señor*, but Father Flynn said he thought, or hoped, he didn't mean it.'

'It's a risk we daren't take,' Drummond decided. 'We'd never forgive ourselves if anything happened to them. Gavin, will your folks pay up? It comes to a hundred dollars for each child. That means your father will have to pay two hundred dollars.'

Two hundred dollars! It was a lot of money. Probably, Gavin feared, more than his father had. And a hundred dollars was probably more than the others who had agreed to foster the children had. How would any of them find that much money? But Drummond was right: they couldn't take the chance the bastards wouldn't carry out their threat. They couldn't let the orphans down.

'I'm sure they will,' he said. 'But they might have to borrow it.'

Drummond waved a hand to indicate that that posed no problems.

'I can ride home and find out.'

'There's not time.' Drummond stopped him. He paced to the window and back. 'They want the money delivered to Wheeler's Canyon by tomorrow.' He glanced at the Mexican, who nodded. 'They won't wait.'

'Wheeler's Canyon?' Gavin repeated. That was a half-day's ride from Northend. It certainly didn't leave much time. He would just have to say yes and hope his father agreed he'd done right. In the circumstances what else could he do?

'Gavin, can you ride out to Everly's farm. You know where it is, don't you? Speak to Everly and his wife. See if they agree. While I speak to the others here in town.'

'All right.' Everly's farm wasn't as far out as the Pruitts. If he was quick and borrowed a horse from the livery it would only take him a couple of hours there and a couple back. 'Mr Drummond?' Gavin had thought of another problem. 'Five hundred dollars is such a lot of money. Is there enough cash in town to make it up?'

Drummond glanced at the safe in the corner of his office. One of his many duties was to act as an unofficial banker for the town's citizens and the outlying farmers; none of whom was exactly wealthy.

He frowned, 'I believe there's more than two

hundred dollars in there at the moment. The rest I'll have to beg or borrow from the stores and saloons. I'm sure everyone will help. They must. Maybe they'll even agree to fund some of the money or maybe we can start up some sort of collection.'

Gavin wasn't convinced. Why should anyone but the foster parents pay for the children?

'There must be some way round this problem,' the problem of finances, 'but I can't think straight at the moment.' Drummond passed a hand over what little remained of his hair and looked at Gavin with worried eyes. 'God, this is so awful. How could it have gone so wrong? I thought I was doing right. Instead . . .'

Gavin put out a hand towards him. 'It's not your fault. If we act quickly it'll all come out right.' He sounded much more confident than he felt. It seemed to him that any number of things could quite easily go wrong. 'Do we know who's taken them?'

'Father Flynn thinks it's the Kelman gang,' the Mexican said.

'It must be,' Drummond agreed. 'Who else would dare do something like this?' He went over to the hook behind his desk and shrugged into his coat. He swung round. 'And who the hell is going to deliver the ransom?'

Both he and Gavin knew it was little use asking Les Smith. The man liked his comforts, he certainly didn't like facing up to dangers. He would say that as town constable he couldn't be expected to leave the town to go gallivanting across country to Wheeler's Canyon.

Gavin took a deep breath and said, 'I will. I know the way.'

'Oh no, not you.'

'Someone has to.'

'What would your parents say?' Drummond was obviously thinking that the Pruitts had already lost two daughters, they wouldn't want to lose their only son as well.

'They'd agree it's something I must do.'

'Well, if you're sure? But, Gavin, it could be dangerous.'

'Quite frankly, Mr Drummond, I'd quite like the opportunity to go up against these outlaws for what they've done.'

'Gavin, we all feel angry about this.'

Anger didn't begin to cover what Gavin felt.

'But remember these men are ruthless killers and they won't hesitate to kill. You must promise you won't do anything stupid.'

TEN

Cobb was up when dawn was little more than a streak of pink in the sky. Although he made a grumbling Neil and a tired Sister Catherine get up once the coffee had boiled and they set out soon after, he wasn't happy with the lack of progress made during the day.

He didn't have to worry about Sister Catherine who was proving to be a good rider. The problem was with the wagon. The further into the hills they went the harder and, despite Neil's best efforts, the slower it became for the wagon to follow the trail. It was steep in places, twisted precariously through rocks and brush, was blocked by cottonwood trees. Difficult enough for horses, almost impossible at times for the wagon. Once it did become impossible and they had to backtrack and make a lengthy detour to come out further along.

'Couldn't we leave the wagon behind?' Neil asked when they made a stop to rest the animals and have

70

something to eat. His arms ached and he was covered with sweat from the effort of controlling the two horses.

'I've been thinking the same,' Cobb admitted. 'It would make sense except we'll need it for the children and perhaps for Mary Joseph.' He lowered his voice so Catherine wouldn't hear as he added, 'We don't know how the kids have been treated. They might be hurt. And we don't know how far in front of us they are. We leave the wagon here, it could take us some while to get back to it. Do you want me to spell you driving it?'

'No, it's OK.' Neil shook his head. That would mean he'd have to ride with Sister Catherine. Driving the wagon meant he could stay in the rear. 'Mr Cobb, do you think they are a long way ahead of us?'

'I don't know. I hope not. But we haven't seen any sign of dust or smoke from a fire. That could just mean they're being careful or perhaps they've made a run for some place. It depends on why the gang snatched the kids.' Which Cobb still couldn't figure out. 'Perhaps when we catch up with Mary Joseph she'll be able to tell us more.'

But so far the nun hadn't appeared on the trail.

'I should never have let her remain out here on her own,' Catherine said more than once. 'At the same time she insisted and she's a nun who's taken her vows, not a novice like me. I had to do what she ordered.'

'Don't worry, she must be all right.' Cobb tried to

comfort her. 'She's still leaving pieces of her habit for us to follow.'

Wheeler's Canyon. Kelman thought it was perfect for their purposes. Deserted, desolate. High cliffs on either side. A sandy trail twisting through the rocks. One easy way in, a narrow way out at the far end so they couldn't be trapped. Places where a watch could be kept, both for pursuit and, more important, for the person bringing the money from Northend.

'I doubt anyone'll be here before tomorrow,' he said to Worley as they took their ease round the fire. 'It'll take 'em time to collect the money together and decide who's goin' to be brave enough to bring it out to us.'

'What we goin' to do if they don't pay up? We ain't going to bother to take the kids to the mines are we?' Which would mean a long and tiresome journey. 'Or kill 'em?' Worley didn't mind killing people, in fact he liked it, but he thought he'd draw the line at murdering innocent and helpless children.

' 'Course not.' Kelman felt the same, even if there had been times during the ride here when their crying and complaints, especially those of the littlest girl, had seriously got on his nerves. 'If by some chance the good people of Northend don't pay but, Brad, I bet they will, we just leave the kids here and ride for Mexico. They'll be found sooner or later.' And if they weren't – hard luck.

*

It was getting late and Cobb thought they'd have to make camp for another night when Catherine let out a screech.

'There she is! Look! There!' She raised herself in the stirrups and waved wildly. 'Sister Mary Joseph! We're here!'

'Hush.' Cobb rode over to her and caught her arm.

'What's the matter?' Startled Catherine looked at him. 'Mary Joseph is safe.'

'The outlaws might be nearby.'

'Oh.' The girl collapsed back into the saddle, putting a hand to her mouth. 'I never thought of that. They didn't hear me, did they? I'm sorry.'

'No harm done.' Or at least Cobb hoped not. He turned to look down the slope of the hill.

Sister Mary Joseph, a small figure dressed in black, was visible against the brown of the rocks where she was sitting. Thank God she was all right. The nun heard their approach and stood up, waiting for them to reach her.

'Sister, Sister!' Catherine threw herself from the horse and ran to the other nun, flinging her arms round her. Tears of relief came into the girl's eyes. 'We've found you. You're safe. Oh, how are you? Are you all right? Oh, I've been so worried.'

'Sshh, I'm fine.' Mary Joseph said. She was lying, for it seemed every part, every bone, every muscle of her body ached, hurt and protested. 'But you shouldn't be here! You should have remained at the mission. I'll speak to you later.' She pushed Catherine away and, putting hands on hips, turned to stare at Cobb. 'You took your time in getting here.'

Her sharp tone and words hid the relief she felt at their arrival. She wanted to scream with joy and hug them all but it wasn't in her nature to give in to her emotions.

Cobb opened his mouth then closed it again, for once at a loss for words, making Neil grin.

'And now you are here you must be quiet. The outlaws are just beyond the ridge.' Mary Joseph pointed to the hill behind her.

'What are they doing?' Cobb asked.

'Making camp,' was Mary Joseph's surprising answer. 'They look as if they're stopping here for quite a while.'

'Out here?' Cobb looked round. There didn't seem to be anything here to stop for. 'Sister Catherine, can you look after Mary Joseph?' He ignored the older nun's snort of derision. 'While me and Neil go and see.'

'Be careful. They've posted a look-out. Over there.'

Cobb had to admire the nun, she hadn't missed anything. Keeping to the cover of the rocks, he and Neil made a slow way up the side of the hill. He wondered if he might find she was wrong but when they reached the top and peered into the canyon it was obvious she was right.

An untidy camp sprawled below. A fire was lit, the horses unsaddled and secured in a rope corral. And the men were lounging around the fire, a couple of them fast asleep. It was obvious they weren't here just for a short stop. He couldn't imagine what they were up to.

'Look, Mr Cobb, there's the kids.'

The five children were sitting, together, against the rocks. To Cobb's relief they didn't seem to be hurt. One older boy had his arms round a little girl and the other three were holding hands.

'Can we go down and rescue them?'

Cobb looked up at the sky, which was rapidly darkening into night. 'It's too late. Be too risky going down into the canyon when we can't see what we're doing. We could slip, have an accident. Alert the bastards. We'll have to wait until morning so we can scout the place out first.' He wanted to plan the rescue properly so nothing went wrong.

When they returned to the nuns, Mary Joseph was sitting in the wagon trying not to show her annoyance as Catherine fussed around her.

'Sister, have you any idea where we are?'

'Not exactly no, Mr Cobb. But I'm almost sure we're only a few miles from Northend.'

'The town where the kids were going?' This was becoming more and more surprising.

'Yes. It's certainly in the direction the outlaws have taken. More to the north but not far away. And by the way they're children, not kids.'

'Er, yes, sorry.' Cobb went red. 'I wonder what the hell they're waiting for?' He blushed again because he'd said 'hell' in front of two nuns.

Mary Joseph, who'd heard much worse, took no notice. 'They seem to be waiting for something. Or someone.'

'Yeah, but who?'

*

It was late evening before the $500 was gathered together. By then most of Northend's citizens knew what was going on and several of them had crowded into Drummond's office. They were all angry, demanding action. Constable Smith had wisely absented himself in case they demanded action of him.

'Instead of paying the bastards, we oughtta go after 'em. Shoot the sonsofbitches.' That was Everly, the farmer, who had accompanied Gavin back to town.

'Rescue the kids,' someone else added to murmurs of agreement.

'No, no,' Drummond raised his hands, trying to calm things down. 'We're talking about the Kelman gang and we know they're all killers.'

'There's more of us than there are of them.'

'We must consider the orphans as well. We don't want them getting hurt in any crossfire.'

'Mr Drummond is right,' Gavin sided with the mayor. 'Once I've paid the ransom and the kids have been freed, that's the time to go after the outlaws.'

Everly spoke up anxiously, 'We will do that, won't we? I can't afford to lose a hundred dollars without at least trying to get it back.'

'Don't worry,' Drummond said. 'They won't get away with what they've done. But it's no use going off half-cock. Like I said, this is the Kelman gang. We do anything without thinking about it we risk being shot.' He stared round at the other men, satisfied that they agreed with him. 'Now, Gavin, he put a hand on the young man's shoulder, 'it's too late for you to ride out to Wheeler's Canyon tonight. Go, get some rest. Be up early.'

'Yes, sir.'

'And good luck.'

Gavin nodded. He thought he might need all the luck in the world.

ELEVEN

'Good luck, Gavin,' Drummond repeated the next morning. 'And be careful.'

It was very early. The two of them were alone in the livery stable, which was lit by a single oil-lamp.

'The money is all there,' Drummond went on, patting the saddlebags. 'I counted it out myself. There shouldn't be any trouble but don't take any chances. Do whatever the outlaws want.'

'Yeah, I will,' Gavin promised. He swallowed nervously and swung up into the saddle.

Drummond reached up to shake his hand then hurried to open the stable doors.

Gavin rode out into the dark, empty street beyond. It was still cool but he knew that wasn't the reason why he shivered. He was nervous . . . no, admit it, terrified. The Kelman gang. They had quite a reputation – a bad one – and here he was about to ride into their camp. He wondered if he'd be allowed to ride out.

Well, someone had to do it and he'd volunteered.

There was no turning back, no changing his mind. He was glad his parents didn't know what he was doing but he hoped they would understand and approve.

He reached the end of the street and looked back. Drummond remained where he stood, a blacker outline against the stable. The mayor raised his hand in a salute and then as Gavin turned the corner he could no longer see the man. He was completely on his own. He kicked the horse into a steady lope.

From their small hiding place in the rocks, Sister Catherine looked up at the ridge obscuring Wheeler's Canyon from view. She sighed and said, 'Oh, I do hope the children are all right. The poor things. They must be so frightened. I hope they're being given enough to eat. I wish we could see them. I wish they knew we were close by.'

'Sister!' Mary Joseph cut across the younger nun.

Catherine turned away, blushing. Neil felt sorry for her. Mary Joseph might be older and more experienced but that didn't mean she had to be so sharp and impatient with someone who couldn't help being younger and a little naïve.

'I presume, Mr Cobb, you're not going to sit around all day but do intend to rescue the children?'

But then, Neil thought hiding a grin, Mary Joseph was sharp and impatient even with someone as experienced and worldly wise as Zachary Cobb.

' Yeah, I do, but we must do it right.' Clearly Cobb

didn't like being criticized but, rather in awe of the nun, was trying not to show it.

'We mustn't risk the children being hurt,' Catherine added.

Mary Joseph ignored her. 'Did you make any plans during the night?'

'Sister Catherine is right. We certainly don't want the men using the children as shields.'

Catherine gave a little cry of horror.

'Unfortunately they've chosen a good place to camp. There's no easy way to reach them without the danger of being spotted. And it's no use going in shooting. There are six of them and only Neil and me.' And Neil wasn't a particularly good or accurate shot. 'I've been thinking that maybe the best bet would be to approach from the upper end of the canyon. If we're able to.'

'Won't they have posted a guard there?'

'They might but there doesn't seem to be a guard posted anywhere except for the one looking towards the trail leading to where you think Northend is. It's as if they don't expect anyone will be coming after them, or at least not this quickly . . .' which confirmed Cobb's view that most outlaws were possessed of few brains '. . . but are expecting someone from the town. Neil.'

'Yes, sir?'

'Let's climb the ridge and look at their camp, make sure they're not getting ready to pull out and then we'll go and find out what the canyon is like further along.'

It was soon clear that the gang wasn't going anywhere, not for a while anyway. A new fire had been lit, the horses were still unsaddled and the men were enjoying a cooked breakfast; something, much to Neil's annoyance, Cobb hadn't allowed in case their fire was spotted.

Neil glanced back over his shoulder and said, 'Mr Cobb, Sister Mary Joseph wants us.'

The nun was waving wildly. Now what?

Cobb and Neil slithered down the slope to where she and Catherine waited by the wagon.

'What is it?'

'I took a walk to the Northend trail,' Mary Joseph said. 'Don't worry,' she added quickly as Cobb frowned, 'I made sure I wasn't seen. But,' she pointed towards the slope that twisted down between high walls, leading to the valley below, 'someone's coming.'

'What? Who?'

'I don't know. But he's coming pretty fast.'

'Could it be whoever the outlaws are waiting for?' Neil suggested.

'Maybe.' That seemed most likely. 'Or it could be one of the outlaws who's been to the town for some reason. Let's go and find out. Maybe we can stop him.'

'Is that a good idea?' Mary Joseph asked.

'Yes,' Cobb said shortly. He didn't like anyone telling him his business nor having to explain himself but as the nun stood there obviously waiting for an explanation, he was forced to go on, 'If he is from Northend we need to know what Kelman is waiting for. If he's a member of the gang and we capture him he'll not only be one less to deal with but he can tell us what the gang is up to.'

'We're coming too,' the nun decided.

Cobb opened his mouth to object.

'He'll be here soon,' Catherine said urgently.

Reluctantly Cobb realized there wasn't time to argue and thought it probably wouldn't do much good anyway. Mary Joseph was just about the most stubborn person he'd ever come across; almost more stubborn than he was!

'OK, but let me go about stopping him in the way I want. This is no time to be gentle.'

As usual Mary Joseph had the last word. 'Don't worry, Mr Cobb, I know that sometimes harsh action is unavoidable. I don't always approve but I shan't interfere.'

Gavin knew he was nearing Wheeler's Canyon. That it was just beyond the next high ridge of rocks and trees. He wished his heart wasn't beating quite so fast or that his hands weren't quite so slippery with sweat. He had the money. There couldn't be any danger. . . .

Danger came before he expected it. As he slowed the horse to take a turn in the steep slope that took him out of sight of the ridge, a man suddenly stepped out from the rocks straight into his path and waved his arms in the air. The animal squealed in fright and reared. Taken by surprise Gavin was sent tumbling from the saddle to land with a painful thump on the ground. When he sat up he saw two men standing over him. They both had their guns out, pointed straight at him.

He gulped and said to the elder of the two, 'Are you Kenny Kelman?'

Cobb glanced at Neil. At least that meant this young man, younger than Neil, wasn't a member of the gang. Neither did he look like an outlaw. As far as Cobb could see he wasn't even carrying a weapon. All the same he wasn't about to take any chances.

'Stay where you are. Who are you? What are you doing here?'

'My name's Gavin Pruitt. Are you the ones got the kids? I've got the money if you are.' Gavin nodded at the horse. 'You can let them go.'

'Money?'

'Yeah. You are members of the Kelman gang, ain't you?' But suddenly Gavin didn't sound too sure. Then he caught a glimpse of two women wearing black habits – nuns! – in the rocks. Were they prisoners as well? What was going on here? Who else could these men be?

'No. Are you?'

'Of course not. I'm from Northend. My folks are going to foster two of the children.'

'Pruitt! Yes!' Mary Joseph stepped out into the open, followed by Catherine. 'Mr Cobb, that was the name of one of the families. I don't believe this young man poses any threat.'

'I've already worked that out.'

'You and Neil can put your guns away. Let him up and see what he has to tell us. You can trust us, Mr Pruitt, Mr Cobb here is a private detective.'

Gritting his teeth against Mary Joseph's advice and interference, Cobb reached out a hand to help Gavin to his feet: 'What's this about money?'

Gavin glanced around at the four of them. 'The youngsters have been kidnapped by the Kelman gang. They're demanding a five hundred dollar ransom for their release. I'm taking it to them.'

TWELVE

So, that was what this was all about! Cobb felt relieved to find out.

'A ransom!' Mary Joseph declared furiously. 'How dare they use children like that. It's outrageous. Mr Cobb, what now?' She sounded as if she would like Cobb to ride into the outlaw camp all guns blazing.

'The money must be delivered and soon,' Gavin said urgently. 'They threatened to kill the kids otherwise.'

'Oh no,' Catherine cried. 'Oh no, they wouldn't.'

'Well I doubt that they would,' Cobb agreed. 'But with people like Kelman you never can tell.' Catherine shook her head in denial but no one took any notice of her. 'Gavin, do they know who's going to deliver the money?'

'No, sir. The message came from Father Flynn at the mission. None of the gang has been to Northend.'

'OK. In that case I'll take the money into the camp.'

'Oh, I don't know.' Gavin felt he had to protest whilst being secretly relieved.

'I'm paid to take risks. You're not. And that way I can see for myself what's going on.'

Mary Joseph said, 'Remember, Mr Cobb, the children are of prime importance. Any heroics like capturing the Kelman gang can come later.'

'Yes, Sister, I know,' Cobb said crossly but he didn't say any more because he knew the nun was very worried about her charges. 'I shan't do anything to put the children's lives in jeopardy.'

'Do you want me to come with you?' Neil offered.

'No,' Gavin said. 'The message was for one man to go alone. And unarmed.'

'It's all right. You four go back to the wagon. Wait there.'

'I wish you luck, Mr Cobb,' Mary Joseph said. 'Please take care.'

'And please bring the children safely back to us,' Catherine added, twisting her hands together.

Cobb nodded and mounted Gavin's horse. He handed his gun to Neil. He wasn't happy about riding into the outlaws' camp without a weapon but he could see no alternative. He might be searched and he didn't want to do anything to anger them, at least not while the children were still their prisoners. He waited until Neil had ushered the other three back amongst the rocks where they couldn't be seen, then gigged the horse into a walk. He had almost reached the top of the slope when the outlaw keeping watch stood up.

As Cobb drew the horse to a halt, the man waved his rifle and challenged him, 'You from Northend?'

'Yeah.'

'Ride round to the top of the canyon. Camp ain't far in. We'll be waiting. Don't try nothing stupid.'

Cobb had to admire the place Kelman had chosen for his camp. Just inside the mouth of the canyon anyone coming from that direction would be seen straight away. Rocks lay scattered all round the bottom of the canyon for shelter. Otherwise the walls were sheer and would be difficult to scale.

As he rode slowly forward two men came closer to meet him. They were both in their twenties and he guessed one of them was Kenny Kelman.

The other four spread out round the two leaders, so, however fast and accurate he was, if he had a gun that was, he couldn't have got off enough shots to kill them all before being shot himself. It was obvious they'd done this sort of thing before and knew they could depend on one another.

He took a quick glance at each of them. There was another young man with long hair and a black moustache and two slightly older: one completely bald-headed, and the one who'd been in the rocks had grey hair and a long grey beard. The fourth was very young, hardly out of his teens. They all looked hard and quite capable of using the guns with which they bristled.

Not that he was here to force any sort of confrontation, even if he could. He was here to secure the release of the captives. His eyes sought them out. They still waited by the rocks where he and Neil had spotted them the evening before. While the eldest boy and girl – Sister Catherine had said their names were Ernesto and Isabella – both looked at him with hope in their eyes, the other three seemed so worn out and frightened they didn't take any notice of him.

'Get down,' Kelman ordered. 'And don't try no funny tricks. Joe, get one of the kids.'

Grinning, the black-moustached man went over to the children. He snatched at the littlest girl but Ernesto knocked his hand away.

'Not her, *señor*, she's too small.'

'Then I'll just have to take your sister, won't I?' Joe pulled an unresisting Isabella to her feet and marched her back over to near where Kelman stood. He held her in front of him.

'Now, mister, you do try something, that little gal is right there in the firing line.'

'There's no need for that,' Cobb said as calmly as he could. 'I'm not about to go up against you.' Despite the pleasure it would give him. 'I'm just here to deliver the money.'

Isabella stared at him and he could see tears of fright in her eyes. He thought it quite likely these men had threatened the children more than once with being hurt or killed if they didn't behave. Perhaps had actually hurt them. He didn't think he'd ever felt so angry or helpless. He clenched his hands into fists and glanced at the girl and quickly across at Ernesto, giving them both a little nod, hoping to convey that everything would soon be all right. He wasn't sure that either believed him.

'You got our money then? The good folks of Northend paid up?'

'Yeah.'

'Done told you they would, Brad.' Kelman slapped Worley's arm and they grinned at one another. 'Let's see it then. It ain't I don't trust you, it's just that I wouldn't trust my own ma where five hundred dollars was concerned.'

The others all laughed.

As Cobb turned to take hold of the saddle-bags, Kelman said, 'Careful. Slowly.'

Obviously he hadn't got to lead a gang by taking anyone's word for what they were or weren't going to do.

'Open 'em up and count the money.'

Cobb hunkered down and tipped the money out on to the ground. His heart sank a little. The $500 was made up of notes and coins of all sorts of amounts. Mostly small sums. It would take him some time to add it up when all he wanted was for this to be over and done with.

But at last he'd finished to Kelman's satisfaction and Worley scooped it all up into the saddle-bags and quickly stepped back again.

'So now I can take the children?' Cobb glanced across at them. Ernesto was sitting up straight, his body tense, hands clenched by his sides.

'Well, now see, here we have a slight problem.'

Cobb's heart missed a beat. What did Kelman mean by that? He didn't like this. Didn't like the way Kelman drawled his words or stared round at the other members of his gang with a cocky smile or the way they smirked back as if they knew something Cobb didn't. Certainly didn't like the way Ernesto slumped back on the ground with a defeated air.

'What are you talking about? What problem? You've got the money you asked for. Five hundred dollars. The deal was you'd then let the kids go. Come on, let 'em go.'

'The *problem*, mister, as I see it is that there's five hundred dollars there but there are six of us—'

'It's what you damn well asked for.'

Kelman scowled angrily, clearly not liking to be interrupted. 'And while Northend is meant to be a poor place—'

'It is.' Another interruption.

'Yeah, mebbe, but see how easily and quickly its citizens gathered together so much.'

'Not easily.' Cobb was liking this less and less.

'So what I propose is that you good people find another four hundred dollars—'

'Hey now!'

'which will give us a nice tidy sum of a hundred and fifty dollars each. Enough to enjoy the bright lights of Mexico for a while.' Kelman looked round at his men again, all of whom were nodding and grinning broadly. Yet again this was working out well as far as he was concerned. 'And so much easier to divide up.'

'You should have thought of that before.'

'I'm thinking of it now.'

'You can't.'

'Yeah, I can and do.'

'The people . . . we . . . we'll never find that much.'

'Oh I think you will, or who knows what might happen to these poor little kids? I'm sure you wouldn't like any harm to be done 'em.'

'You sonofabitch.' It would have given Cobb great pleasure to launch himself at Kelman and punch that smug smirk off his face. It took him all his effort not to.

'Now, now! Time's awasting. You've got till this time tomorrow. So if I were you I'd scuttle back to Northend and begin rattling your collection tin.'

And Cobb, aware of Ernesto staring at him and of Isabella bursting into tears, could do nothing but mount the horse and ride away. The outlaws' laughter rang in his ears.

THIRTEEN

Sister Mary Joseph's wimple was pushed askew. A sure sign to anyone who knew her that she was furious. She stamped up and down, hands clenched at her sides. Neil thought she was a bit like Cobb when he lost his temper and noted that Catherine was keeping out of her path in the same way he was keeping out of Cobb's.

Gavin was distraught. 'How could they do something like that? I thought I was going to take the kids back with me. I can't believe they dared ask for more money.' He frowned and sounding very worried went on, 'It was difficult enough raising five hundred dollars. I'm not sure whether it'll be possible to raise another four hundred. It's almost as much again.' He was certain his father wouldn't be able to give any more. 'God, what are we going to do? Still I suppose we'll have to try.'

Cobb put out a hand, stopping the young man in his pacing. 'No. Wait.'

'No? What do you mean, no?' Catherine cried. 'We must do what they want. Think of the children.'

'The gang will never be satisfied with whatever we give them. They'll always be demanding extra.'

'You can't possibly know that,' Catherine objected. 'They'll surely be satisfied with nine hundred dollars, goodness me that's a fortune! Especially as they must realize the people of Northend won't be able to pay any more.'

'I don't think we can pay even that,' Gavin said.

'Exactly. And then what?' Cobb stared round at them all. 'Perhaps they'll let the children go. Perhaps they won't.'

Catherine said, 'They won't hurt them.'

'Maybe not. But what's to stop them taking the children somewhere else and blackmailing another town into paying money in return for their safety?'

'They wouldn't.'

'But they already have.'

'Hush,' Mary Joseph told Catherine as it looked as if the girl was about to object again. 'Mr Cobb is right. I'm not sure myself that this Kelman will ask for even more money but then I thought the bastard—'

'Sister!' Catherine exclaimed.

'—would be satisfied with his original demand, which was quite bad enough. It's not a risk I'm prepared to take. So, Mr Cobb, what do you propose?'

'I'll have to rescue the children.'

'Oh, but they might be hurt,' Catherine began then fell quiet as the other nun glared at her.

'Do you think that's wise?' Mary Joseph asked.

'I don't know.' Cobb looked down at the ground and sighed heavily. 'But I'm not happy about letting Kelman call all the shots. Who knows what else he'll come up with? And, Sister, I'm not sure how long the children can cope with being the gang's prisoners. They must be terrified, wondering what's going to happen to them. Then after thinking they'd be set free, they haven't been. It might be too much for them to take.'

Mary Joseph nodded.

'But they could be hurt in any rescue attempt,' Catherine said again. 'I'm sorry, Sister,' she added as Mary Joseph seemed about to interrupt, 'but it's true.'

'I promise to be as careful as possible.'

'We don't have any choice,' Mary Joseph decided. 'I agree.'

'I want to help,' said Gavin.

'No, Neil and me can manage. You should ride back to Northend. Let them know what's going on. I don't want anyone from there riding out to see where you are and perhaps getting in the way. Anyway the gang might be watching out for whoever came from Northend to ride back.' Cobb paused, frowning.

'What's the matter?' Gavin asked.

'You'll have to keep amongst the rocks till you're far enough away they won't spot the difference between us.'

'OK.'

'You'd best be on your way.'

Despite wanting to remain and help, Gavin knew Cobb was right. He swung up into the saddle. 'I wish you luck. Bye, Neil, Sisters.' And digging his heels into the horse's sides he rode out towards the trail leading down the hill.

'What now?' Mary Joseph asked.

'Now? Now, we wait.'

'Wait?' Catherine screeched. 'What for?'

'Till it's dark,' Cobb explained patiently. 'Now I've seen what the canyon is like it's no use hoping to be successful by riding into it in the daylight. We need the cover of darkness. Come on, Neil, let's ride to the far end of the canyon and scout it out.'

'Gavin said there was a way into it from that end,' Neil said.

'Good. Let's find it.'

Neil went over to saddle the horses. To his embarrassment Catherine followed him.

She obviously wanted someone friendly to talk to. For as she handed him a horse blanket she said, 'Sister Mary Joseph is always finding fault with me. She doesn't like me.'

'Perhaps it's not that,' Neil said awkwardly. 'Perhaps it's because she's worried about the children.'

'No.' Catherine shook her head sadly. 'She's been abrupt with me all along. Even though I've only tried to do my best. I really wanted to come on this journey, help with the children. I love children. But she's made it miserable for me.' The girl sighed. 'I know I should accept her criticism and not mind. But I do. And it makes me wonder if I'm cut out to be a nun. Yet it's something I've always wanted to be ever since I was a young girl.'

Neil wasn't sure what to say. She looked so unhappy, so unsure of herself. 'Maybe now, with so much going on, ain't the time to make any decision. Especially one you may come to regret. You should wait until all this is over. Perhaps talk it over with someone you trust.'

'Yes, yes, you're right.' Catherine's face lit up with relief, making her prettier than ever. 'Thank you, Mr Travis, you've been a great help.'

Feeling light-hearted, Neil waited for Cobb, and they rode out together. It took them a long time to work their way round to Wheeler's Canyon's far end. Here the rocky walls sloped down towards a narrow entrance, beyond which the trail turned and twisted.

Cobb rode a little way into the canyon before returning to where Neil waited.

'What do you think?' Neil asked.

'It should be all right. Once in the canyon there's room to manoeuvre so if we are seen and the gang start shooting we can turn round and ride out, either through the exit or over the rocks.'

'You sound worried.'

'Not worried, but I'm not too keen on approaching the camp without going all the way along the canyon. But it twists and turns so much I can't figure out how to do that without the risk of running into a guard waiting round the next bend.'

'If we go in at night they shouldn't see us.'

'No, but then we won't see them until we're in their camp. Neil,' Cobb turned to the young man, 'you don't have to come if you don't want to.'

'What! Let you take all the glory for yourself?' Neil said with a grin. 'I can see the headline now: "Zachary Cobb singlehandedly captures the Kelman gang!" '

'That's not it. But you're not a Bellington's detective. You're not paid to go up against six outlaws.'

'I want to help those poor kids.'

'OK, thanks. I'll be glad of your company.'

Neil felt very pleased by that. Most times Cobb gave the impression he was a hindrance.

'And, Neil, remember no gunplay unless it's absolutely necessary. Our only aim is getting the children out.'

'Will that be possible without the gang knowing?'

Cobb shook his head. 'I doubt it. The alarm is bound to be raised. I don't see how we can avoid it.'

'So, when the outlaws start shooting at us, what then?'

'You must take the children and the nuns and get them to Northend. Sister Mary Joseph will help you find the way. You shouldn't have any difficulty even in the dark because it looks like there's a reasonably good trail to follow, especially once you reach the valley.'

'What about you?'

'I'll do all I can to delay the gang.'

That's what Neil had been afraid of. Six men against Cobb. Neil sounded worried as he said, 'Wouldn't it be better if I stayed with you?'

'The kids and the nuns are the main concern. You help them. Don't worry I'll be all right. Surprise will be on my side. I won't take any risks.'

Neil could tell the man's mind was made up and, of course, he was right. To a Bellington's private detective the job came first; above personal safety.

'So what do we do in the meantime?'

'Like I said, we wait.'

Worley was troubled. Not about the brats. He knew they were upset, the little girl was crying again and even the eldest boy had stopped glaring at his captors. Had given up. So what? Life was cruel, full of disappointments. They'd have to put up with it.

No, he just hoped Kelman hadn't bitten off more than he could chew. Although $500 wasn't a great deal of money surely, in the circumstances, it was enough. Why ask for more? Especially when it was doubtful the citizens of a place like Northend could come up with it? The longer they waited here the more likely the law would catch up with them.

Worley knew the problem was that what had gone wrong in Santa Fe was still preying on Kenny's mind. Not only was Kenny anxious to re-establish his leadership but he wanted to show he could get the better of mere townsfolk. And while he couldn't do that with the townsfolk of Santa Fe he could with those of Northend.

Not that Worley dared object. The way Kenny was acting you'd think he'd successfully robbed the US Mint. And the others all seemed to agree, greedily wanted more, without considering the risks. Worley couldn't wait until the next day when with, or without, the extra money, they could be on their way. He wanted to reach the safety of Mexico.

FOURTEEN

Waiting was the difficult part. But at last darkness fell and the waiting was over. The moon was almost full, casting an eerie silver glow over the landscape, with no sign of any clouds. But Cobb couldn't do anything about that. They had to go tonight.

'Sister Mary Joseph, you and Sister Catherine wait here by the wagon' – the two horses were already harnessed to it – 'be ready to move. No stopping to hug the children or to find out what happened or where I am. Just grab the kids, get 'em in the back. And go. Sister Catherine, you ride Neil's horse while Neil drives the wagon. Don't bother with the spare horse. Don't wait for anything.'

'Yes I understand.' Mary Joseph asked no questions about what Cobb might be doing. She had her job to do, which was to take the orphans to safety, Cobb had his. If that involved risking his life or shooting and killing the outlaws then so be it.

'Please, please be careful,' Catherine said and

then going up to Neil as he waited by his horse said again, 'Please, Mr Travis, be careful, I don't want to see you hurt. Or Mr Cobb.'

Neil was glad it was dark so no one could see how red-faced he'd become.

'And please bring the children back safe and sound.'

'We will.'

'Come on, Neil, let's go.'

Neil hadn't been with Cobb for long but Cobb knew that in a fight he didn't have to spell out what he wanted done. That even in the heat of the moment Neil would do what Cobb said or signalled. That he could be trusted. To go into a dangerous situation like this with someone like Neil at his side, rather than alone, was something Cobb was becoming used to, was getting to like. Not that he would have said so to Neil, of course.

Once they were in the canyon, its walls looming high and close on either side, Cobb indicated they should dismount and lead the horses. And now as they inched their way along he was glad of the moon lighting their path for without it it would have been difficult to make much out. He reckoned they must almost be at the outlaws' camp, it should be round the next bend, when he heard Neil's gasp, quickly stifled. He glanced towards the young man, who pointed to the rocks.

One of the outlaws, the bald-headed guy, was crouched right there in front of them. Had only to turn his head to see them. Might hear them if they made another move. But make a move they had to, they couldn't just wait where they were.

Signalling to Neil to stay where he was, Cobb stepped silently forward. He'd reached the rocks when the man sensed his approach and stood up. Taken by surprise the man remained still just long enough to give Cobb time to dive forward. They grappled together, falling heavily to the ground, Cobb on top. The outlaw gave a little grunt and quickly Cobb's hand went over the man's mouth preventing him making another sound, other hand grabbing at his gunhand. To his surprise the outlaw made no move, had gone limp beneath him. Was it a trick?

Cautiously Cobb raised himself a little, prepared for an attack. None came. Drawing his gun, ready to bring it down on the outlaw's head, he got to his knees and stared down. The man was dead. With a sense of shock Cobb felt under his head. It was sticky with blood. Reholstering his gun he went back to where Neil waited.

'He's dead. He must have hit his head on a rock as he fell.'

'It ain't your fault.' Neil knew that while Cobb wasn't averse to killing outlaws he preferred to do so in a fair fight. 'He'd have killed you as soon as look at you.'

'I know.' Cobb sighed. 'Let's move on. And hope there aren't any more guards.'

There weren't. And suddenly the camp was just ahead of them. Cobb counted the sleeping bodies:

five. Good, that was all of the gang. No one had been alerted by the short struggle. And the children were still over by the canyon wall. Asleep as well by the looks of it.

'Stay here with the horses,' Cobb whispered in Neil's ear. 'Be ready to move.'

Neil nodded.

Keeping out of the way of the gang's animals, not wanting to spook them, Cobb tiptoed over to the children. They lay together, arms round each other for warmth, for they weren't even covered with a blanket and they were too far from the fire to feel its benefit. He bent down by Ernesto, put a light hand over his mouth and shook him. The boy came instantly awake, eyes widening in fear.

'Sshh,' Cobb said. He paused as one of the other boys stirred. 'I'm here to get you out. Will the rest be quiet?'

Ernesto shrugged. 'I hope so, *señor*.'

So did Cobb. He glanced back at the outlaws. No movement. 'Help me.'

Carefully Ernesto got to his knees and reached for his sister while Cobb caught the arm of the boy who had stirred. Jaime's eyes opened but he made no sound. Cobb thought: this is going to be all right. They might get away without alerting the outlaws.

That was when the little girl woke up. And screamed.

'Quiet,' Cobb said urgently while Ernesto said, 'It's all right, Maria.'

They were too late.

'Hell and damnation!' That was Kelman leaping to his feet. 'What the hell's happening?'

'Mr Cobb.'

Neil's cry of warning was drowned as Kelman went on, 'The kids! Someone's there. Get 'em!'

Neil drew his gun, firing wildly at the outlaws. He didn't aim at anyone, his only hope being to pin them down. At the same time he dragged the two horses forward.

Cobb was already moving. He picked up the two boys, one under each arm, leaving Maria for Ernesto. 'Go!' he yelled at Isabella who took to her heels.

Yells came from Kelman and Worley. Shots blazed out of the night but the outlaws were confused, not knowing what was going on, and Cobb and the others were out of the firelight, so they couldn't be seen very well. The bullets went wide.

Neil was already mounted and he leant down pulling Ernesto and Maria on to the horse behind him.

'Isabella!' Ernesto called. 'Here.'

She veered towards them and Neil caught her arms, swinging her up in front of him.

'Get out of here!' Cobb yelled.

Neil didn't look back. He sent his horse galloping forward.

Meanwhile Cobb also paused to fling several shots towards the gang, stopping them coming after him. Catching hold of his horse's reins he threw Jaime and Manuel up into the saddle. 'Grab on!' he told them and brought his hand down hard on the horse's flank. With a squeal it bolted forward and he breathed a sigh of relief as neither boy fell off.

The horse caught up with Neil at the canyon entrance and not wanting it to go in another direction, he reached across to grasp the reins.

'Hold on,' he yelled and swung the animals towards where the nuns waited.

'They're coming!' Mary Joseph turned from where she was looking up the hill, beyond which came the sound of shooting. 'I can hear them. Get ready.'

'Yes, Sister. Oh, I do hope everything is all right.' Catherine's hands were clutched together. 'There.'

Two horses appeared over the top of the ridge coming full tilt towards them.

Breathlessly Neil pulled the horses to a halt by the wagon. Isabella fell to the ground but was up and moving towards Mary Joseph without making a sound. The nun didn't pause but lifted her up, practically throwing her into the back of the wagon before grabbing Maria from Ernesto. As Ernesto didn't need help, Neil bundled the other two boys into the wagon.

He passed the reins of his horse to Catherine and, hoping she could manage on her own, clambered up on to the seat. 'Everyone all right?'

'Yes, yes!' Mary Joseph cried out.

Neil brought the reins down on the backs of the horses and the wagon lumbered forward. He risked a glance back. As far as he could make out there was no pursuit but, alert to danger, he kept the horses moving at as fast a pace as he dared, hoping that he didn't miss the trail. Catherine seemed to be having some trouble with her horse but he didn't wait for her, knowing she could catch up and before long she had done so.

Mary Joseph looked round at her charges. They were white-faced, scared, a crying Maria cuddled on her lap.

'You're all right now. You're safe.' She hoped she was right and she too looked back. Nothing and no one. Not even Mr Cobb. He was giving them time. The sound of firing was slowly dying away the further they travelled.

'Truly, Sister?' Ernesto asked. He clutched at Isabella's hand and then said, 'There, Jaime, Manuel, did you hear that? Sister Mary Joseph has saved us. I told you she would. That we could trust her.'

Tears pricked at the nun's eyes and she quickly blinked them away.

'But where is Mr Cobb?' Catherine cried out. 'We must wait for him.' She pulled her horse to a stop in front of the wagon, forcing Neil to come to a halt. 'He's on foot. He might be shot. Hurt. We must go and see.'

'You heard what he told us,' Neil said. 'We were to take the children to Northend.'

'But—'

'Move out of the way, Sister,' Mary Joseph ordered. 'Mr Cobb knows what he's doing.'

Reluctantly Catherine did so. 'Aren't you worried

about him? Mr Travis, how could you leave him behind?'

Neil didn't reply. Of course he was worried. But he was even more worried about what Cobb would do to him if he disobeyed orders.

Mary Joseph turned her attention back to the children. They seemed much calmer now, accepting that their ordeal was at last over, that they would soon be with their foster parents. All except Maria. The little girl was weeping and it seemed like she would never stop. Then Mary Joseph remembered.

'Look what I have for you,' she said. She reached into her pocket and, with a flourish, pulled out Maria's rag doll.

'Mine,' Maria said and took it from the nun, cuddling it to her chest. 'Dolly.' And not only did she stop crying but her face lit up and she smiled a gap-toothed smile.

That was when Mary Joseph was glad of the dark. For this time when tears came into her eyes she could do nothing to stop them running down her cheeks.

FIFTEEN

Once the children had gone, Cobb, continuing to shoot at the gang, dived for the shelter of the nearest rocks. Ducking down behind a couple of large boulders he swiftly reloaded his gun and took stock of the situation.

One of Neil's wild shots had struck home. The very young outlaw lay unmoving on the ground, legs twisted underneath him. If he wasn't dead he was at least out of the fight. That left four. They were milling about, yelling at one another, confused. That wouldn't last long. Kelman would rally them. They would come after him. He might be able to beat all four, he might not. To stay here in the rocks invited being shot.

'The kids have gone,' Worley called out to Kelman, who nodded.

The sensible thing was to let them go, they had their money, didn't need the children any more, but just then Kelman was way beyond acting sensibly. 'We've gotta get 'em back. Get the horses. We'll go after 'em.'

Cobb saw the two men running for the horses. He didn't want them getting away or, worse, going after the children. In the wagon Neil wouldn't have been able to get far enough away yet to escape them and he'd be no match for the outlaws. He stood up. The long-grey-bearded man was coming towards him. He paused to aim and fire, having considerable satisfaction when the man doubled over and collapsed. Then Cobb raced out of the rocks.

Kelman was freeing the horses from their rope corral. The animals were already nervous. Cobb fired over their heads, shouting at the same time. A couple galloped away.

'Hell!' Kelman grabbed at the nearest horse. 'Who the hell is out there?'

'There!' Worley pointed.

He fired several times. Cobb flung himself to the ground and rolled away.

With a little shock Worley realized that now one rider had taken the kids, they were being attacked by just a lone gunman. He didn't dare tell Kelman that. He'd be furious. So was Worley. One man was responsible for all this damage. It must be someone good: two men were dead. Probably three. But there were still three of them, they should be able to manage one man! At the same time he could be the law and while he was alone now perhaps other lawmen or a posse were on the way. And while that wasn't likely Worley wasn't thinking straight. He was spooked. He just wanted to get away.

He went up to Kelman, clutching his arm. 'Forget

the kids. Let's get outta here.'

'No.'

'Kenny, it's stupid. They've gone. Let 'em go.'

'Yeah, c'mon, let's go.' That was Joe, firing towards where he'd last seen Cobb.

But Cobb was no longer in the same position. Beyond the light of the fire he was running towards the other side of the canyon. On his way he almost tripped on something lying on the ground. Cursing he looked down. His curses changed to a smile as he saw it was the saddle-bags. Bulging still. He paused to grab them up and continued for the rocks. By the time he reached them, the three remaining outlaws had managed to catch their horses. Without bothering to saddle them, they mounted up and sped away.

Cobb stepped out into the open, raised his gun, supported his wrist with his other hand, aimed and fired. With a little cry Joe flung up his arms and toppled off his horse. The other two didn't pause in their flight.

Cobb ran over to the remaining horse. The animal was jittery with fright and would have run but its feet were trapped in the rope that had formed the corral. Cobb caught hold of its mane, calming it down until he could free it. Making sure he kept hold of the saddle-bags he vaulted on to its back and started after Kelman and Worley.

'Dammit!' Kelman yelled. 'He's coming after us.'

Worley glanced back over his shoulder. 'He can't

catch us up.' He sounded more hopeful than certain.

'Sure he can. Or maybe he can't.' Kelman brought his horse to a halt and leapt from its back.

'What the hell are you doing?' Worley had no choice but to stop as well.

'Making sure the bastard don't do any more to us.' Kelman drew out his revolver, waited until his pursuer came within range and pulled the trigger several times. The horse tumbled forward and the rider was pitched headlong off, hitting the ground hard. 'Got him!'

As Kelman was inclined to go back to see if the man was still alive, Worley said, 'Don't bother. Even if he ain't dead, he can't follow us no more. He might have friends nearby.'

'OK.' Kelman was reluctant, he thought they should make sure, but he could tell Brad was in no mood to do anything but ride. And he was probably right, it didn't matter.

All the breath knocked out of his body, Cobb was forced to lie still for a few minutes. When he could, he sat up, drawing out his gun. He came up into a crouch, staring round. But the outlaws weren't coming to finish him off. He saw them outlined, a blacker shadow against the black sky, before they disappeared over the rim of the hill.

He knew he was lucky, had been lucky all along, with the odds stacked against him. Somehow the fight had gone his way and now the two remaining outlaws were running from him. He stood up, intending to go after them. Only to find he couldn't. The horse had been shot and was dead.

'Damn and blast!' Cobb yelled in frustration.

All right, four members of the Kelman gang were either dead or badly wounded and could be taken into custody. But Kelman and his second in command had escaped. Would surely head for Mexico where the law couldn't reach them.

But, Cobb suddenly grinned, they would go there without their $500!

By the time the wagon reached the valley the sky was gradually lightening and Neil decided he could slow down. There was no sign of anyone coming after them. Neither was there any sign of Cobb but he tried not to think what that might mean. He glanced round. The children were asleep. Mary Joseph smiled at him, the smile lighting up her otherwise severe face.

'It shouldn't be long now,' she said. 'I seem to recognize this valley. I for one shall be glad to reach Northend so the children can recover from their ordeal. And so Sister Catherine can do the same.'

Neil looked at the young nun, who kept peering along their back trail as if anxious to see Cobb. Her face was drawn, lips pinched. He wished he could comfort her and quickly turned his thoughts from that direction.

'You've done well, Mr Travis, thank you.'

Neil smiled. Mary Joseph was as sparing with her compliments as Cobb; it was all he would get.

Early morning, the town of Northend came into view. Mary Joseph woke the children and they sat up, eager to see their new home. She told Neil to drive into the main plaza where she knew Mayor Drummond had his office.

Neil had hardly brought the wagon to a halt when the door to the real-estate office opened. Several people led by Drummond and Gavin Pruitt rushed out.

'They're here! The children are here!' Drummond yelled and other men and women emerged from several of the stores. 'Safe and sound. At last.'

'You're OK. Everyone OK?' Gavin asked as he reached them, then with a quick look round added, 'Where's Mr Cobb?'

'He stayed behind.' Neil jumped down from the seat and went round to the back to help lift the children out.

There were 'oohs' and 'aahs' from the crowd, who pushed forward, wanting to see properly. Now they were here, surrounded by people, the children stood shyly, trying to get behind one another. They were overwhelmed by the excited and friendly faces, everyone asking questions, demanding to know what had happened. Maria looked as if she was going to start crying again.

'Mr Drummond,' Mary Joseph pushed her way forward, 'these children have been through such a lot. It would be best if they were removed from public gaze.'

'Of course, of course,' Drummond agreed. 'Bring

the dears into my office until we sort everything out. Come along, children.'

Catherine helped him usher them on to the sidewalk.

'Sister,' Neil said from Mary Joseph's side. 'I must go back and search for Mr Cobb.'

'Yes,' she nodded. 'Don't worry, you can leave everything here to me.'

Neil didn't doubt that.

'And don't worry too much about Mr Cobb. The fact that he didn't come after us probably just means he couldn't catch his horse and was left afoot.'

'I hope so.' Neil turned to Gavin. 'I'll need a fresh horse.'

'There'll be one at the livery. Neil,' Gavin added as the young man started to move away. 'Neil, would you like me to come with you?' He was torn between doing what he thought was right and remaining here to get to know Ernesto and Isabella. And going home.

Neil wasn't too sure about accepting Gavin's help. This was Bellington business. Cobb might not like it. But Cobb wasn't here and Neil had no idea what he would find at Wheeler's Canyon. If it was Cobb's dead body then he didn't want to be alone when he discovered it.

'Yeah, OK, thanks.'

'You go down to the livery, start saddling up a couple of horses while I tell Mr Drummond what I'm doing. Are you hungry? Would you like breakfast before we go?'

Of course Neil was hungry. He always was. It was an indication of how worried he was that he said, 'No, I'd rather be on my way.'

SIXTEEN

'Rooms are ready for you both and the children at the hotel, ' Drummond told Mary Joseph once the office door had been closed on the crowd outside and it was quiet. 'They can wash, change out of those dirty clothes and rest up. Or have something to eat.' He smiled at the five children who stood lined up against the wall as if for his inspection. 'Thank goodness none was hurt. We couldn't believe the news when the messenger from Father Flynn arrived.'

'No, well, it's over now,' Mary Joseph said sharply, not wishing the children to be reminded of their ordeal. 'Sister Catherine, perhaps you would take them to the hotel, see to their needs.'

'Of course.' Catherine nodded.

'You can rest as well while you're there. It's been a long night. A long few days. You look tired.'

'I am,' Catherine admitted. 'What about you? You must be tired too.'

Mary Joseph was but she was scared that if she

lay down she wouldn't want to get up again and she still had a job to do.

'First, Mr Drummond, I must visit the children's prospective foster parents. Talk to them.' Discover if they were suitable.

'Right at this minute?' Drummond sounded doubtful.

'After all that's happened it's important to settle the children as soon as possible.'

'Yes, I suppose so. Most of those concerned are here in town. And I've sent to Gavin's parents so they wouldn't worry when he didn't return home. They might come in today or tomorrow.'

'Good. Although I shall also need to see the people at their homes.' Make sure they were suitable as well.

'They know that. I'll put everything in motion.'

'Thank you. The rest of you go on over to the hotel and I'll see you later.'

'All right, Sister. Come along, children.' Catherine took hold of Maria's hand. 'You'll soon be in your new homes. Won't that be wonderful?'

As they went out, Mary Joseph turned to Drummond. 'Someone should ride to Father Flynn. Tell him everything is all right. He'll be worried.'

'I'll see to that as well. Here, Sister, sit down.' Drummond pulled his chair out from behind the desk. He was afraid that if the nun didn't sit down she would fall down. 'It's awful, isn't it, that people should try and take advantage of innocent young kids. It's so unfair. And then when Gavin came back and said they were demanding another four hundred dollars!' He shook his head. 'I'll tell you here and now we could never have raised that much more.'

'Did you try?'

'Well, no,' Drummond admitted, a little uncomfortably under her stare. 'I knew it would be no use. Now, you take it easy for a while and I'll get the hotel to send you over something to eat and drink.'

Mary Joseph leant back in the chair and closed her eyes. She only meant to close them for a few moments but she was almost instantly fast asleep. Drummond tiptoed out of the office, leaving her alone.

Before long, Kelman and Worley stopped to rest and take stock. Neither man could believe what had happened: that they were alone, with the rest of the gang, four men, being either dead or captured. The children rescued. Even worse, although they wouldn't admit it to each other, both knew there had been no good reason why they'd run. Allowed one man to drive them away. They'd panicked. And that had never happened before. It wasn't enough of an excuse that their attacker was a good shot. They should have stayed and made a fight of it.

'We can't go into Mexico like this.' Kelman came to a halt in his pacing up and down. 'We can't go anywhere.' He pointed towards the horses. 'Hell, we ain't even got saddles or bridles. Or canteens. We ain't got our rifles or any of our gear. We ain't got nothing. And, Brad, we especially ain't got the five hundred dollars.'

'I hope you ain't goin' to blame me for that.' Worley was scared. He'd never seen Kelman in such a terrifyingly bad mood, when he was likely to do anything.

But Kelman said, 'No, it weren't your fault. Nor mine.' He wasn't about to admit responsibility. 'It just got left behind.' His eyes took on a crafty glint. 'It oughtta still be there in the camp along with the rest of our stuff. We're goin' back for it.'

Worley hesitated. He didn't want to go back. Supposing the law had reached the camp by now? Supposing the man who'd attacked them wasn't dead and was there searching through their belongings? Supposing . . . well, supposing anything really. On the other hand Kenny was right. They had nothing with them except what they stood up in. A few coins in their pockets. Which wouldn't get them far. They couldn't get any money unless they found someone to steal it from . . . but $500 was back at the camp just lying around waiting to be picked up.

And $500 to share between just the two of them was $250 each. Enough to last a long time while they took it easy in a Mexican brothel. With that sort of money they could have all the Mexican whores they wanted. Whereas without it they wouldn't get any sort of welcome at all. Surely, there wouldn't be any risk, not if they were careful.

'Well?' Kelman barked.

And did he really want to argue with Kenny while he was like this – no!

'OK.'

Buzzards flew over Wheeler's Canyon. Neil found his heart beating fast as he and Gavin approached it. What would he do if Cobb was dead? It would be little consolation he'd died doing his job. As they rode into the canyon mouth and the camp came into view he saw no sign of any horses, not even Cobb's – did that mean the outlaws had escaped? No, that wasn't right. There were bodies lying on the ground. How many?

'There are three here,' Gavin said.

Was one of them Cobb? Neil's heart missed several beats as he looked at each of the bodies and then missed several more as he realized that, no, none of them was Cobb.

'There should be another one in the rocks just beyond the next bend,' he said.

'I'll go see,' Gavin said and added in an attempt to reassure Neil, 'It looks like Mr Cobb is OK.'

Neil nodded. He couldn't see a reason for Cobb to be in any other part of the canyon except here where the main gunfight had taken place. But then where was he?

'Be careful,' he called after Gavin, getting off his horse to examine the ground.

When Gavin came back he said, 'Yeah, there's another one further along. What shall we do? Should we bury 'em?'

Neil hesitated. He didn't like the thought of leaving the bodies out here in the open, where they would be prey to buzzards and wild animals. But they were dead and couldn't be helped. Whereas Cobb, although alive, might need help.

'It'll take too long,' he decided. 'Besides, we ain't got a spade and the ground is real hard.'

Gavin nodded. He was quite happy about not having to dig four graves. 'When we get back to Northend we can tell the undertaker and he'll come out here and collect them.'

'Gavin, there are two outlaws missing.'

'Do you think Mr Cobb has gone after 'em?'

'Knowing Mr Cobb, yeah!' Neil's grin hid his worry. In that case, two against one, Cobb could still have been shot. He swung back up on to his horse. 'Let's get on. Find him.' The trouble was he was no good at tracking and he didn't imagine Gavin would be either.

'The bastard ain't here,' Kelman said. 'I done told you we should've made sure he was dead. If we had we would've seen whether he had the saddle-bags with him and could've taken 'em from him.'

They were at the place where Kelman had shot the horse and their pursuer had fallen off.

They had already been to Wheeler's Canyon. Ignoring the bodies of the men who'd once ridden with them they'd searched the camp from top to bottom. Searched amongst the rocks. Searched up and down the canyon. The saddle-bags and the $500 had gone.

Kelman decided their attacker must somehow have both. There was no other explanation. So after saddling and bridling their horses and collecting up whatever they could find a use for, they'd ridden back to the site of the ambush. The animal still lay there, dead, but of their pursuer there was no sign.

Kelman now stood, hands on his hips, a faraway look in his eyes. 'If he ain't kept the money for himself, he must be taking it back to Northend.'

Oh-oh.

'So, Brad, that's where we're off to. There won't be no risk,' he added quickly as Worley opened his mouth to object. 'There ain't no law worth spit in Northend. And no one'll be expecting us so we'll have surprise on our side. We've gotta get our money back and, more important, take our revenge on that bastard for what he's done to us.'

Kelman obviously wanted no arguments. And in the circumstances Worley didn't give him any.

SEVENTEEN

'There he is!' Gavin pointed. The figure was little more than a speck showing dark against the grey-green slope of the hill but his sharp eyes had picked him out.

'Wait,' Neil said as his companion started to head in that direction. 'Let's make sure it is Mr Cobb and not one of the missing outlaws.'

But a few minutes later they both recognized the private detective. With a little cry Neil sent his horse galloping forward.

'Mr Cobb!' he called out as he and Gavin rode closer.

Cobb, whose feet were aching, he was most definitely not used to walking, came to a relieved halt and waited for them.

'Are you OK?' Neil said, jumping off his horse. 'Are you hurt?' He would have liked to put his arms round Cobb but he held back, knowing the man wouldn't appreciate that. 'What happened?'

'I'm all right,' Cobb said, except for several

bruises where he'd fallen off the horse. Neil didn't need to know about them. 'What about the kids?'

'They're safe in Northend,' Gavin said.

'Thank God.'

Neil said, 'We've been to Wheeler's Canyon. Four of the outlaws are dead.'

'But Kelman and one of the others escaped.' It was something Cobb didn't like admitting, it sounded like a failure to him. 'I was chasing after them but they shot the horse out from under me. Left me on foot.'

'They're probably on their way to Mexico,' Gavin said, not worried about them any more.

'Yeah, I guess.' Cobb looked at Neil. 'Thanks for coming out here to look for me so quickly. You've done a good job.'

Neil went red with both pleasure and surprise. It wasn't often Cobb praised him; criticism was much more likely.

'We'd better get on back to Northend. Give these to Mr Drummond.' Cobb turned to pick up the saddle-bags which he'd put on the ground behind him when he didn't know who was approaching.

Gavin's eyes widened. 'Is that the money?'

'Yeah,' Cobb said with a grin. 'All five hundred dollars of it.'

There were times Neil wondered how Cobb made such a success of being a private detective and this was surely one of them. The kids rescued, most of the outlaws killed – *and* the money recovered! How did he do it?

He mounted his horse and held out a hand to help Cobb on behind him. Now to get to Northend and have something to eat. He was starving.

'We'll wait till tonight to go in,' Kelman said as he and Worley came to a halt by a stand of rocks and cottonwood trees a little way away from Northend. He didn't want to wait but he didn't want anything more to go wrong and it seemed senseless to take another chance by riding into the town when it was daylight and they might be seen.

Worley nodded agreement. 'If we don't strike lucky right off we give it up, right?'

'Yeah.' Kelman was anxious to get his hands on the $500 and also to shoot the bastard who'd stolen it from him but he wasn't a fool. Money could be stolen from other people and they'd passed a couple of lonely farms on their way here. Places which wouldn't be guarded, would be easy to rob.

They settled down to wait out the afternoon.

'What's the matter, Mr Cobb?' Neil could almost hear the man thinking. 'You seem worried.' He couldn't think what there was to be worried about, not now.

'I am. Who knew about the kids coming to Northend?'

'The nuns . . .' Gavin began.

'Apart from them.'

'What do you mean?' Neil asked.

'I can't believe that the Kelman gang just

happened to be in the right place at the right time to grab the kids and hold them for ransom.'

Neil thought about that but still couldn't see what Cobb was getting at.

'It could have been a coincidence,' Gavin suggested.

But Cobb had never liked coincidences and he shook his head. 'I think someone told them.'

There was a moment of silence then Gavin said, 'But who? Who would or could have done something like that?' He sounded disbelieving.

'Think about it,' Cobb said. 'The gang are chased out of New Mexico and just happen to ride to this area of the desert, when they could have gone absolutely anywhere. Why come here? There's nothing here for them. Why not head straight for Mexico? Except, they get here at the same time as the children are travelling to Northend. Have the gang kidnapped anyone before? Or have they always just been bank and stagecoach robbers?'

'I don't know,' Gavin said.

'Nor do I,' Cobb agreed, wishing he could contact Bellington's and see what was on their files about the gang. But he thought he would have heard if Kelman had been into kidnapping, which was a more serious and unusual crime than robbery.

'But who could have told them?' Gavin repeated his question.

'Not anyone who's been involved with fostering Mexican orphans before.'

With a frown of thought Neil said, 'That lets out

the two nuns and Father Flynn.'

'Father Flynn would never do anything like that,' Gavin added.

'Gavin, has anyone in Northend ever been involved with fostering before?'

'Not as far as I know.'

'Not even any of the farmers or ranchers?'

'I don't think so.'

'What about Paul Drummond? Did he mention doing anything of the sort before, perhaps somewhere else?'

'No.' Gavin paused. 'Mr Cobb, you don't really think he could be in with the gang, do you?'

'I'm sure someone is. Tell me about him.'

Gavin thought for a moment or two. He didn't really want to tell Cobb anything, it seemed disloyal to Drummond, but supposing Cobb was right?

With a little sigh, he said, 'He's been in Northend for a long time. In fact he was one of its founding fathers as it is now. I mean for years, even before the Civil War, there's been some sort of trading post on the spot, a couple of saloons. They served the miners in the hills and travellers from the mission on their way to Colorado. But a few years ago ranchers and farmers started to move into the area and it was soon obvious that the town would have to grow to cater for all the newcomers.'

Cobb nodded. That was happening all over. 'Do you know where he came from?'

'Yeah. New York. Although he's been out here for quite a while. The story goes he put up money of his own to help the town and then to help himself he started up the real-estate office in an effort to sell more plots of land.'

'Is he successful?'

'Well, I suppose he is one of the town's wealthier citizens. But then the town isn't very wealthy so that doesn't mean he's rich.' Gavin paused, then a bit reluctantly went on: 'There are several jokes going the rounds about him.'

'Oh?'

'First off that his wife spends his money as fast as he earns it. That she forced him to stand for mayor, although if that is true he certainly enjoys the position now he's got it. And that he's always starting up schemes to get rich but they never amount to much.'

'So perhaps he hasn't got as much money as he pretends or would like?'

'Maybe.'

'And he could need more, especially if he feels he has a certain life style to maintain.'

'Yeah,' Gavin agreed, 'but even so I really can't see him doing something like this. He seemed so anxious about the children.'

'We'll see.' Cobb had been doing his job long enough to take no one and nothing at face value. 'What about the people who agreed to the fostering? Could one of them be involved?'

'Apart from me and my parents?' Gavin said with a grin then immediately turned serious. 'No, they couldn't be. They're just ordinary people. Like me and my parents! And remember it was Drummond who approached us, not the other way round.'

'In every case?'

Gavin frowned. 'I think so.'

'Mr Cobb,' Neil said, 'if you're right, about Drummond or someone else, are the kids still in danger?'

'I hope not. I shouldn't think so, especially if Kelman and his cohort are on their way into Mexico. I doubt Drummond could act on his own and kidnap the children without the help of the gang.'

'Will you be able to prove he's involved?'

'I'm certainly going to try.'

EIGHTEEN

'Well done, Mr Cobb, well done!' Drummond shook Cobb's hand. 'You not only recovered the children but our money as well. What a relief. I didn't think we'd see that again. Well done.' He took the saddle-bags from Cobb and went over to the safe. He unlocked it, put the saddle-bags inside and shut the door with a little clang. Standing up, he rubbed his hands. 'They can remain in there until I get the chance to sort the money out and give it back to those kind folks who donated it. Now, Mr Cobb, is there anything I can do for you?'

'Where are the two nuns?' Cobb asked.

'Young Sister Catherine is looking after the children over at the hotel. Although I think that once they'd had something to eat they all went to bed and have remained asleep ever since.'

'And Sister Mary Joseph?'

Drummond smiled. 'After a short rest, she's been busy, visiting with the foster parents, making sure they're suitable.'

'And are they?'

The mayor looked a little put out, as if Cobb shouldn't have any doubts seeing as how they'd been approached by Drummond in the first place.

'She hasn't found any fault with them,' he said shortly. 'And, Gavin, unless your folks come into town she wants to ride out with you tomorrow to your place.'

'Sure.'

'I think she's finished for the day and has also gone to the hotel.' Drummond paused then asked Cobb, 'What are you going to do now? I mean, with your job done will you be leaving us?'

'With all that's happened I'd better stay around for a few more days.'

Cobb looked hard at the man, trying to judge his reaction, whether he was cross or pleased. It was difficult to tell, although he did sound startled as he said, 'You don't believe there'll be any more trouble, do you?'

Cobb shook his head. 'No, not really. But it'll be best to make sure.'

'Of course, yes, of course, I understand. You can get rooms at the hotel. Now would you and your companion, Neil isn't it?' Drummond turned to Neil with a little smile, 'like to come home and have dinner with me and my wife?'

Neil didn't care where he had dinner or with whom, just so long as he had dinner soon.

'Thanks for the offer,' Cobb said but he had no intention of eating with someone he might have to arrest. 'It'd be best if we went over to the hotel. It's been a hard few days. We're both tired.'

'Fine, all right. Perhaps I'll see you tomorrow?'

Cobb thought Drummond could count on that because tomorrow he was going to start investigating the man. He went outside with Neil and Gavin.

'What about you, Gavin? I guess you'll have to stay in town if Sister Mary Joseph wants you to take her to your folks' farm tomorrow.'

'I would anyway. It's too late to start for home tonight.' Gavin looked up at the sky which was already darkening into evening. He was quite happy about that. It would mean another night spent with Cindy. She would probably see him as some sort of hero! 'I'm heading for the Star. Perhaps I might see you there later on?'

'Maybe. Depends on what time we finish eating.' Cobb doubted whether he would feel like visiting the red light district. He was too weary and as for Neil the young man was almost asleep on his feet. 'But if not we'll see you in the morning.'

'OK. 'Night, Mr Cobb, 'night, Neil. I'm glad it turned out right.'

'Time to go.' Kelman nudged Worley awake with his foot. 'It'll be dark soon.'

Worley stood up and stretched. 'What do we do when we get there?'

Before, they'd always ridden into a town as part of a gang. Had reliable men at their backs. And mostly he and Kelman had scouted out the place before

robbing it. Now they were going in alone, not knowing anything about Northend.

'We'd better leave our horses at the livery or iffen
that's shut mebbe outside one of the saloons.'
Kelman was obviously thinking the same. 'Then
walk round the town, get an idea of its lay-out. See
if we can find out where the money is. And that
bastard.' He grinned. 'Or if not, perhaps there'll be
somewhere else we can rob.'

'Mebbe we can do that anyway.' Worley grinned
back. 'If they can raise five hundred dollars there's
sure to be some rich pickings.'

They mounted up and urged their horses out of
the trees. The road leading to Northend was nearby
and before long the lights of the town came into
view.

Cobb was disappointed that neither of the nuns was
in the hotel dining-room but according to the clerk
on duty they'd eaten earlier and then gone to their
rooms. Cobb didn't want to disturb them. He was
also disappointed that there was only one bedroom
left, the hotel not being very big, which meant he'd
have to share with Neil, although he was thankful
there were, at least, two beds.

The hotel didn't have much choice in food either;
it was either beef stew or steak and baked potato,
followed by apple pie. They both chose the steak and
were pleased that it was well cooked and plentiful.

By the time they'd finished and drunk a couple of
cups of coffee Neil was yawning almost constantly

and Cobb just hoped that nothing happened to stop them getting a good night's sleep. He couldn't think what might but when working as a private detective it was best not to take anything for granted.

It was dark when Ernesto woke up. He was sharing a room with Jaime and Manuel and they were still asleep in the other bed, both breathing steadily. He was fed, washed and rested. And happy. Quietly, so as not to disturb his friends, Ernesto got out of bed and went over to the window, peering out on to the plaza below.

Although it was late most of the stores were still open and quite a few people were about, women and children as well as men who might otherwise be on their way to the cantinas. By the light of lamps hanging in the store windows he could see the well where a couple of young women were talking. It all looked very exciting.

Ernesto was no longer tired. He couldn't stay here in this room any longer, not when there was so much to explore. He decided to get dressed and go out and walk round his new home. Knowing if he was seen he would be stopped he went down the rear staircase, letting himself out of a door near the kitchens. It opened into a yard at the back of the hotel. Opposite, a door in the wall surrounding the hotel was open. He went out and walked round to the plaza.

It was pleasantly warm and all about him people talked and strolled. They looked friendly and healthy and well off, not like the poor Mexicans in the town near where he'd lived with his parents. As for the many different goods for sale in the store windows he could hardly believe his eyes! It was wonderful.

He knew better than to go alone and at night into the red light district, where the men might be rough, but he eventually found himself in a quiet part of the town, with no one else around. He was about to retrace his footsteps when he saw the livery stable. It was still open and he decided to go inside for a quick peek. He loved horses and almost wished he, instead of Manuel, was being taken on to help the owner, although Isabella wouldn't have a place here as the man only wanted one boy to help with the saddling and bridling. And he didn't want to go anywhere without Isabella, for she was the only family he had left.

Ernesto suddenly heard movement in the rear of the stables. He looked up, hoping that if he was seen he wouldn't be in trouble. And came to a startled, frightened halt. A man stood in one of the stalls and Ernesto recognized him at once. It was the bad man who'd kidnapped him and the others. The boy swallowed his gasp of horror and dropped down into the stall nearest to him which luckily was empty. Had the bad man seen him? Please, don't let him have, Ernesto thought, feeling very, very scared. But he didn't think he had because no alarm was raised.

Carefully he inched forward and peered round the wooden partition. No, the bad man was still in the same place. And Ernesto realized the man wasn't alone. He was talking to two others. What was he doing here? Did he mean him and the other children more harm?

Ernesto wondered what he should do. Should he find someone to tell?

The bad man laughed and said, 'C'mon, Brad, let's go rob the place. You wait here,' he said to the third person.

Ernesto slipped silently back into the shadows of the stall. If someone was going to wait here, that meant he couldn't do anything but hide even though the bad men were going to do more bad things.

As the two people with Kelman stepped into view going with him to the stable doors, with a feeling of disbelief Ernesto recognized them both.

NINETEEN

Kelman and Worley walked quickly towards the plaza, doing nothing to draw attention to themselves. Not that they were afraid the citizens still abroad would fight back. What had happened in Santa Fe was unusual and Northend wasn't Santa Fe! It just seemed better to steal the money without anyone being any the wiser. They ducked down a narrow alley which led to another alley running along the rear of the stores.

Kelman came to a halt by a door at the end of the row. 'This should be the back of the real-estate office.' He reached out, turning the knob. 'Locked.' He glanced round. Although there were other doors and windows here, most of the places were in darkness and it wasn't likely anyone would look out and see them. 'Let's break it open.'

The lock was flimsy. A couple of kicks and the door flew open, banging back against the wall.

'Hurry,' Worley urged.

They slipped inside without any alarm being raised, finding themselves in a storeroom.

'The safe is in the office,' Kelman said, remembering what he'd been told. 'Should be through here.'

The inner door wasn't locked and they went into the office, pausing for a moment to allow their eyes to become accustomed to the darkness.

'There it is,' Kelman pointed. 'Brad, go on over to the window, keep watch.'

'OK.' Worley stood at the side of the window, peering out. The plaza was gradually emptying of people as they went home for their dinner and the stores shut up for the night. No one was on this side of the square as the places here were already closed.

Kelman knelt in front of the safe, staring hard at it. 'Damn, I can't see nothing. Can we have a light?'

Worley looked at the window. 'No, there ain't no shades or shutters. We'll be seen. Can you open it?'

'Don't know.'

In all his years as a safe robber, Kelman had never had to actually unlock one. Always before there had been a clerk to threaten into doing it for him. This had a combination lock and he didn't know the combination. He had no idea how to listen out for the tumblers clicking into place and it would be almost impossible to come up with the correct combination. If he tried they could be here all week.

'Oh hell.' He lost what little patience he possessed and stood up drawing his gun.

'What the hell do you think you're doing?' Worley asked in surprise. 'Someone will hear us.'

'Too bad,' Kelman said and throwing caution to the wind fired his gun.

The lock broke, the safe door flew open and there were the saddle-bags.

'Hell! C'mon, Kenny, let's go.'

Les Smith knew most of Northend's citizens didn't think he made much of a town constable but he considered he did a reasonable job, especially considering no one else wanted the post. Of course, he did try to avoid trouble and he did take kickbacks from the saloon owners, but at the same time he made sure the stores were secure at night and there hadn't been a robbery here since his appointment. He couldn't see what people grumbled about.

He was on his way round the plaza, testing doors and windows as he did every night, when he heard a gunshot.

Gunshots weren't common in Northend and the few there were usually occurred on Saturday nights in the red light district. This came from close by. Others had heard it. They were pointing towards this side of the square, others were staring at him. Obviously expecting him to find out what it meant.

Smith's heart sank. He could hardly plead sudden deafness or say he wasn't in the vicinity of the shot, not if he wanted to be elected again. And the position was too convenient and too capable of being exploited for him to want to give it up. Perhaps the shot was an accident. . . .

He walked towards the end of the plaza. And as

he neared it, the door to the real-estate office burst open. Two men rushed out. They almost barged into him.

'Hey there!' he cried.

One of the men turned towards him. Smith clearly saw the excited glint in his eyes. It was just about the last thing he did see. The man raised his hand. In it was a gun. And he shot Smith once, twice. The constable was picked up and thrown down again, to land half on the sidewalk, half in the dust of the street. He was dead before he got there.

Someone screamed. A man yelled.

Worley drew his gun and along with Kelman fired towards the townsfolk who were on the other side of the well where the dry-goods store was still open for business. There were more screams and shouts and everyone scattered.

Keeping up a steady fire, the two outlaws raced back for the business district. No one went after them.

'You can have the bed over by the wall,' Cobb told Neil. It was the smaller of the two and didn't look very comfortable.

'OK,' Neil said and began to take off his coat.

And at that minute a shot rang out. Followed by a piercing scream. And then a number of more rapid shots.

'Oh hell, what now?' Cobb exclaimed angrily and went over to the window. He was just in time to see two men running away and other people gathering around a body lying in the road. His heart sank, this wasn't something he could ignore. 'We'd better go on down, see what it's all about.' He hoped it was just an argument between two townsmen and he could let the town deal with it.

Reluctantly he went out of the room and reluctantly Neil followed him. Neil wanted to go to bed, he wanted to go to sleep; he was only glad their dinner hadn't been disturbed, he couldn't have stood that!

By the time they got to where the body lay, quite a crowd had gathered. Others were coming at a run.

'What's happening? What's going on?' Mayor Drummond was pushing his way through to the front. 'Oh my God, it's Les.' He turned to find Cobb and Neil at his elbow. 'Les Smith is, I mean was, our town constable.'

'Who saw what happened?' Cobb demanded of those nearest to him.

'We heard a shot,' a miner said. 'Then when Les went to see, two men came out of the real-estate office—'

'At a run.'

'—And one of the bastards shot Les. They didn't give him no warning or nothing.'

'Not even a chance to draw his gun. Just shot him dead.'

'Then they ran off.'

'Mr Cobb!' Drummond came out of his office, ashen-faced. 'The money has gone.'

'Kelman and his cohort,' Cobb said with a quick

glance at Neil. 'It has to be. They escaped me and instead of going to Mexico came here.' He sounded both annoyed and upset.

'It wasn't your fault,' Neil said.

'No indeed, Mr Cobb,' Drummond added. 'You did a good job.' He paused then asked in a puzzled tone, 'But how did they know where the money was kept?'

'That's something I'll ask when I catch up with 'em.'

That meant they were going chasing off after them, Neil thought. Tonight. Right now. He hid a moan.

'We'll start out at once and, Drummond, you see if you can raise a posse.'

'Yes.'

'Mr Cobb! Mr Cobb!' The crowd parted for Sister Mary Joseph. She looked worried and upset, her wimple askew as if she had just shoved it on any old how.

Cobb reached out a hand towards her. 'Kelman has been here. He's shot the constable and stolen the money.'

But the nun shook her head as if to say she wasn't worried about that. Breathlessly she said, 'It's Sister Catherine! She's missing from the hotel.'

'Are you sure?'

'Yes. I'm afraid those men must have taken her as a hostage!'

TWENTY

Ernesto hid in the stall, burrowed in the straw, scared he would be spotted as Sister Catherine paced up and down by the stable doors. Not that she looked like Sister Catherine any more. She wasn't wearing her habit, for one thing, but had on a divided skirt and checked shirt under a thick jacket. Her hair hung loose. She even had a gun buckled on her hip!

Ernesto found it hard to believe the nun had anything to do with the bad men who'd kidnapped him and the others. But, of course, it was true. Had to be true. She certainly wasn't here against her will.

And what would she do if she discovered him and realized he knew her secret? Ernesto didn't think she would behave like the friendly, concerned girl she had been on their journey from the nunnery in California. Then she had been so anxious about them, wanting them to go to happy homes. The boy came to the sad conclusion that that could only have

143

been so she could accompany them and somehow let the bad men know where they were.

Tears came into his eyes. He'd liked Sister Catherine much more than the severe Sister Mary Joseph, of whom he'd been a little afraid. But she had deceived him, deceived them all.

It seemed like forever that he lay where he was, not daring to move, hardly daring to breathe, hoping the straw didn't make him sneeze and immediately feeling like he wanted to sneeze. After a long, long while he heard what sounded like shots in the distance. Catherine must have heard them too, for she cursed, swore! and went into the rear of the stable, leading three horses to the door. Three horses, not two, Ernesto saw, wondering what that meant.

Within minutes the two bad men came into view running hard down the street.

'What's happened?' Catherine shrieked in a most un-nunlike manner.

'We were seen,' Worley gasped. 'Had to shoot someone. A lawman.' He leant forward, hands on knees, trying to get his breath back.

Catherine didn't seem upset that someone had been hurt. 'And Cobb?'

'Didn't see him,' Kelman said. 'Pity, but we'll have to forget about him. Get outta here. We've got the money.' He hefted the saddle-bags into view and Ernesto saw Catherine smile. 'That's the main thing. C'mon, Cathy. Let's leave this hick town behind. Head for Mexico. You'll like it there.'

And the girl made no objection as he boosted her up into the saddle of one of the horses. He mounted another. Worley was already on the third. Without any further talk they galloped down the road.

Shaking, feeling sick Ernesto stood up, brushing himself free of the straw. What should he do? He had to tell someone. But who?

Knuckling tears out of his eyes, Ernesto started back towards the plaza. Panicking, he lost his way and almost ended up in the red light district. He had to retrace his steps. This time he reached his destination. And he found a great commotion going on, people shouting and pointing, rushing to and fro. He stood alone on the corner, scared all over again, no one taking any notice of him.

Suddenly he saw Sister Mary Joseph being escorted into the hotel by the man called Drummond. In relief he took a few steps towards them before catching sight of the nun's face. She had always looked so strict, so in control, now her face was creased with fear. She didn't even seem angry with the man for holding her arm.

Ernesto wondered if she was worried about him because he wasn't in his room. Was she cross with him for leaving the hotel when he should have been in bed asleep? So cross she would part him from Isabella, make him go back to the nunnery? And would she be so cross she wouldn't believe him about Sister Catherine but would punish him for telling lies?

What was he going to do? What?

Then Ernesto caught a glimpse of the young man who was going to be his brother. Gavin, his name was. He was coming in this direction. Ernesto thought, hoped, he could trust him. And he stepped out of the shadows in which he was hiding.

Gavin came to a startled halt. 'Ernesto!' he exclaimed. 'What are you doing here?'

'I'm sorry, *señor*,' Ernesto said as politely as he could. Then all his fears came bubbling to the surface and clutching at Gavin's coat, he gabbled, 'Sister Catherine has gone with the bad men—'

'Yeah, we know. She's been taken as a hostage. But,' Gavin reached out to catch hold of the boy's arm, 'there ain't no need for you to worry. You go on back to the hotel. We're setting off after her.'

He gave Ernesto a little push, anxious to get down to the livery and start saddling horses for the posse.

'No, no, *señor*,' Ernesto said, bouncing from foot to foot. 'You don't understand.'

'What's the matter?'

'Sister Catherine is not a hostage.' Ernesto's tongue tripped over the unfamiliar word. 'She has gone because she wants to.'

'What?'

'*Sí, señor*, it is true. They were together in the stables. I hide and I see with my own eyes. She is one of them.'

'Oh God.' Gavin didn't stop to think the boy might not be telling the truth, incredible though what he said sounded. Ernesto looked too upset and frightened to be making this up. 'Oh hell! And Mr Cobb and Neil have gone after them.' Thinking that Catherine, like the children, had been kidnapped. They could walk right into a trap. 'Didn't you see them?'

'No, *señor*, I got lost on my way back here from the stables.'

'You must have missed them. Damn!'

Like Ernesto, Gavin didn't know what to do. But he quickly made up his mind. After taking Sister Mary Joseph back to the hotel, Mayor Drummond was going to organize a posse. The last posse to go out after robbers had been a couple of years ago when the town had a proper lawman, a marshal, who'd organized everything. Now their only lawman lay dead and while most of the men present, young and old, were willing to join in the chase they had no idea of what to do, what was needed, where to go. It could be hours before they were ready to ride out. And by then it could be too late for Cobb and Neil.

And if he waited around trying to make Drummond listen to this latest piece of news, to convince him it was true, it would only delay things even more, even if Drummond even believed him.

'What are you going to do?' Ernesto asked as Gavin strode towards the stables.

'Go after Cobb and Neil. I must warn them.'

'Let me come, *señor*.'

'It'll be too dangerous.'

'Please,' Ernesto said, adding craftily. 'I saw which way the bad men went.'

Gavin didn't have time to argue. 'Come on then. Can you help saddle two horses?'

'*Sí, señor.*'

As they started down the road together, Gavin said, 'You've been a very brave boy. I'm very lucky and my parents are lucky too to have a boy like you, and your sister, coming into our home.'

'Thank you, *señor.*'

'And please, Ernesto, don't call me *señor*. My name is Gavin.'

'*Sí, señor.*'

'I hope they don't hurt her,' Neil said.

He was very worried. He'd liked Sister Catherine even though she was a nun and he'd been a bit wary of her in her black habit. He didn't want anything to happen to her and he knew that not everyone would respect the fact that she was a nun. He was no longer tired and even if Cobb suggested they rest, he'd try to persuade him to carry on through the night. Tell him the trail was an easy one, following as it did a good, well-travelled road.

'We'll catch up before they have a chance to do anything,' Cobb promised, hoping that was true.

They were riding in the direction Kelman must have gone: surely this time to the safety of Mexico. But Cobb knew he could be wrong, he seemed to have been wrong about everything in this case, and they could be heading for Colorado or even California. Probably it would have been best to wait till daylight and they'd have had a trail to follow, but then the outlaws could have ridden too far ahead for them to catch up. They just had to take a chance and go this way and hope it was right.

Cobb brought his horse to a halt and got off, searching the ground as well as he could. The moon was still full and it was just possible to make out the tracks of several horses – perhaps three – recent ones too. He hoped they were the tracks of Kelman.

He got back on his horse and kicked it forward. 'What I can't understand is how they managed to grab her.'

'Would they have gone into the hotel?' Neil hazarded a guess. 'Perhaps tried to snatch the kids again?'

'Maybe. Or maybe for some reason Sister Catherine went out for a walk and they saw her and took their chance.' But Cobb sounded doubtful.

Neil glanced across at him, wondering what he was thinking, knowing he blamed himself for what had happened, although no one else would do so. Cobb had done all he could. No one could have guessed Kelman would come to Northend.

He said, 'They also knew where the money was. D'you think Drummond told 'em?'

'Someone did. Otherwise why should they think it was in the real-estate office?'

'They could have forced someone to tell them.'

'Ye-es.'

But Cobb sounded doubtful about that as well. Much more likely they'd somehow met up with Drummond and he'd told them. But if so then why had it been necessary to shoot out the lock? Why couldn't Drummond have given them the safe's combination so they could open it with no one hearing? Even left it open for them? Unless to do so would have been to implicate himself. He shook his head, no point in worrying about that at the moment.

He glanced back.

'Any sign of the posse?'

'No.' Cobb had the feeling it would take some time before anyone started out after them. It was just him and Neil and for once in his life Cobb didn't like it, wished the posse would put in an appearance.

There was something wrong about all this but he couldn't decide what.

TWENTY-ONE

'Honest, Cathy, whatever gave you the idea you wanted to be a nun?' Kelman said, lounging back against a rock. 'You, a nun!' He laughed. 'None of us at home could believe it when we heard.'

Catherine looked at her brother in some annoyance. 'I did want to be a nun. I'd've made a good one too.' Dedicated to looking pale and interesting. 'What I didn't like was being told what to do all the time. And I could have done without Sister Mary Joseph and her sour disposition. She didn't like me and I certainly didn't like her!' She leant forward. 'Anyway, you should be glad I was at the nunnery in California. Remember it was me came up with the scheme of kidnapping those orphans and you needed my help to do it.'

'Much good it did us,' Kelman said grumpily, thinking of the dead members of his gang.

'You and Brad have got five hundred dollars,' Catherine pointed out and, to make sure she received her share, added, 'To split three ways.'

151

'Yeah, no thanks to you. First off you let that damn stupid nun follow us and then you led a private detective, some sort of lawman, right to us. Hell, Cathy, what were you thinking of? You should've stopped the damn lot of them. And why the hell didn't you warn us about Cobb? We could've done something about him if you had.'

Catherine could see her brother was about to lose his temper. Most of the time she loved Kenny, would do anything for him, other times she was wary of how unpredictable he could be, was scared of him.

'I did my best. I tried to stop Mary Joseph following you. And I didn't know about Cobb until it was too late, but I tried to delay him and his idiot helper. It was difficult without giving myself away.'

'OK, OK. I guess it don't matter. Like you said, we've got the money.' Men were always willing to be recruited into his gang and it wasn't like he actually missed any of the others, except perhaps for Joe. 'Would've liked to kill that interfering bastard though.'

It seemed as if Kelman might get his wish. Just at that moment Worley, who was keeping watch from a nearby slope, hurried back.

'Riders coming.'

'A posse?' Kelman jumped up.

'Don't think so. There's only two of 'em.' Worley grinned. 'In fact, it looks to me like it's Cobb.'

Kelman and Catherine glanced at one another and smiled.

'What are we going to do?' Catherine asked.

'Wait for 'em.'

'Wait?'

'Yeah, as if we don't know they're on their way. Let 'em ride in thinking they've got the upper hand and then spring a nasty surprise.' It was a trick Kelman and Worley had pulled more than once. It had always worked before. And Cobb wouldn't come in shooting, not when there was the danger of 'Sister Catherine' getting in the way of a bullet. 'And, Cathy, you can help.'

'How?'

'Put on your habit over your clothes. Pretend you're our prisoner. I'll tell you what to do.'

The girl smiled and hurried to do as her brother said.

It was mid-morning when Cobb, followed by Neil, rode up a sagebrush-covered slope. He signalled a halt. 'Quiet! There they are. They've come to a halt.' He was surprised he was able to get so close to the outlaws' camp without them knowing about it. Surely they'd guess pursuit would come after them, even from a small town like Northend.

'Can you see Sister Catherine?' Neil asked anxiously.

'There she is.' Cobb pointed to the nun sitting on one side of the small fire while the two outlaws sat on the other. 'She doesn't look hurt. Thank God.' He hesitated. 'I'd like to wait for the posse . . .'

'There may not be time for that.'

'I know. I don't want those two bastards making a

run for it and I certainly don't want to risk anything happening to Sister Catherine. We'll have to go down there. Surprise is on our side. And if we ride to the other end of this slope and approach from the far side we can get almost into their camp without being seen.' Cobb thought he was trying to persuade himself as well as Neil it would work.

Neil nodded. He wasn't all that happy about going up against two outlaws who'd shown themselves so eager to fire their guns but he was willing to do it for Sister Catherine.

When they were close by, Cobb signalled Neil to dismount; they would approach on foot.

As they stepped into view, Kelman looked up. He yelled, 'Hey!'

And at the same time Cobb yelled, 'Hold it right there.' And he had his gun out and pointed, aware of Neil doing the same.

'Oh, Mr Cobb!' Catherine cried, leaping to her feet. 'Oh, thank goodness!'

'Stand up the pair of you,' Cobb ordered. 'Take out your guns and drop them on the ground. Now step away from them, hands in the air. Do it!'

Kelman said, 'We're surrendering. Don't shoot.'

'Sister Catherine, they haven't hurt you?'

'No, oh no, but I was so frightened. They threatened me.' The girl moved away from the fire getting in between Cobb and Kelman. She swayed a little so Neil looked at her, hoping she wasn't about to faint.

Unseen by either Cobb or Neil, Kelman quickly reached behind his back for the derringer he kept in his belt, palming it in his hand. Worley already had his Bowie knife stuck in the top of his boot within easy reach. They glanced at one another. This was going to work.

'Neil, get their guns. And be careful.'

Neil went to do so. Starting to sob Catherine moved closer to Cobb, so he half-turned to her, his attention on her, not the outlaws.

'Mr Cobb! Mr Cobb, look out!' Gavin's shout from nearby reached the camp. 'She's in with them.'

Cobb hadn't become the successful detective he was by hesitating. While part of his mind might find it difficult to believe Sister Catherine could be one of the outlaws, another part said act first, consider the arguments later. He acted. He swung a fist at the girl knocking her to the ground.

And saw Worley's hand flash down and come back up holding his knife.

'Neil! Watch it!'

Neil was too surprised to take any evasive action except to swing his body to one side. But he was too close to Worley to prevent him from thrusting the knife at him. The blade struck hard in Neil's ribs. With a little groan he grabbed at the wound and sank to his knees.

Cursing, Cobb shot Worley and flung himself to the ground even as Kelman fired his derringer. He felt the bullet whistle by his ear. As Kelman dived for his Colt, Cobb rolled over and fired twice. Both bullets struck Kelman in the chest, knocking him off his feet. He landed on his back, legs jerking in the dust. Shakily Cobb picked himself up and went over to him, kicking the gun out of the way.

Kelman looked up at him with pain-filled eyes. 'Almost got you,' he said and died.

'Kenny, no!' Catherine screamed and knelt down by her brother's body, catching at his jacket. 'Oh no, Kenny, please!'

Cobb paused only long enough to make sure none of the guns was within her reach, and that she didn't have a hidden weapon, then hurried to Neil. He was lying motionless on his side. A quick glance revealed Worley would pose no threat. The bullet had taken him in the throat.

'Neil!' Cobb turned him over just as Gavin and Ernesto rode up. The wound was deep, was bleeding badly.

Neil moaned and mumbled, 'It hurts.'

'Mr Cobb, are you all right? Oh God, is Neil dead? Ernesto, stay on your horse.' Gavin hastily joined Cobb.

'Help me,' Cobb said and began to tear off Neil's shirt. 'I'll need water to wash the blood away.'

'I'll get it.' Gavin stood up. 'Are the other two dead?'

'Yeah.'

Gavin glanced across at Catherine who was still crying over her brother's body. 'Well, she isn't, so be careful of *Sister Catherine*,' he emphasized the words. 'She was helping these two all along.'

'What are you and the boy doing here?' Cobb asked. He accepted the canteen from Gavin and, pouring water over strips of Neil's shirt, began to wash the wound. 'Come on, Neil,' he muttered. 'Don't die on me now.'

'Ernesto saw Catherine. So we came after you to warn you.'

'You arrived just in time.' Cobb was aware he had been so worried about the girl that Kelman had had the drop on him. Would have shot him. He'd thought something was wrong but he hadn't been alert enough. Had almost got Neil killed by his careless-ness. Was aware that Neil could still die. He glanced down so no one would see the sudden tears in his eyes.

He blinked them away and having done all he could to bandage Neil up, stood up and went over to Catherine. She looked up at him with hate-filled eyes. 'Who was he to you?' He nodded at Kelman.

'My brother.'

'You helped him set this up?'

A change came over the girl's face. It crumpled. 'Only because he made me. I was so scared of him I had to do as he told me. It wasn't my fault.'

'Maybe a judge and jury will believe you but I sure as hell don't.' Roughly Cobb pulled her to her feet.

She gave a little cry and struggled in his grasp, tried to kick him.

Even more roughly he secured her wrists with his handcuffs and shoved his face into hers. 'You'd better pray to the God you were willing to become a nun for that Neil survives because if he doesn't then no judge, jury or God will save you from me!'

*

For once, when Mary Joseph saw Sister Catherine in handcuffs, she was at a loss for words. But not for long.

'I never believed she would make a good nun. She was a very naïve girl who thought it would be romantic to wear a black habit. And of course it isn't. It's hard work. And to think I was fooled by her.'

'If it's any consolation she fooled us all,' Cobb said. 'I never suspected her. Yet I should have done. She was so eager to accompany the children and it was the first time she'd done so, whereas when Neil said neither nun could be involved because they'd done the same thing before I never picked it up. And in her quiet way she did her best to hamper us following the gang. But, Sister, even though she was more or less responsible for what happened, she certainly gave her brother the idea, I don't think she ever meant harm to come to the children.'

'No, maybe not. But I'm afraid I cannot forgive the fact she was prepared to use them for money.' Mary Joseph's voice and face were severe. 'How did she contact her brother? Has she told you that?' The nun couldn't bear to visit Catherine in the jail. Couldn't bear to speak to her.

Cobb nodded. 'Evidently she'd already spoken to him about the groups of orphans and suggested the foster parents might like to pay for them if they were kidnapped.'

Mary Joseph tutted.

'Kelman wasn't interested. At least not until the robbery in Santa Fe failed and he needed what he saw as easy money. Somehow he got a telegraph message to Catherine at the nunnery and she sent a message back saying that a group would soon be on its way to Northend and detailing the journey. Then it was only a matter of Kelman waiting for you to put in an appearance.'

'And when it went wrong?'

'She thought Kelman would go to Mexico and she would go back to the nunnery. At least for a while. Instead Kelman and Worley came here and contacted her at the hotel. And she decided she no longer wanted to be a nun but would go with them. It sounded more exciting!'

Mary Joseph sighed. 'Foolish girl. I suppose Mother Superior would say I should feel sorry for her, that it probably wasn't her fault but was due to her upbringing and the fact she was somewhat simple. I haven't Mother Superior's forgiving nature.'

'At least the children have gone to good homes. Are settling in.'

The nun nodded. She was waiting for an escort to take her back to the nunnery and now she asked Cobb what he was going to do.

'Once I've given evidence at Catherine Kelman's trial' – which was due to be held the next day – 'I have to get back to Bellington's Agency. But on the way I'll call in on Father Flynn, tell him how it ended.'

'He won't believe you. Father Flynn believes only the best of people. You can also tell him I hope to see him again and soon. With more orphans.' Mary Joseph paused again. 'And Neil?'

Cobb smiled. 'He should be ready to travel in a day or two.'

Neil was lying in bed at the hotel, propped up against pillows, taking it easy, enjoying the fuss for once being made of him.

'That's good. He's a nice young man.' Mary Joseph looked shrewdly at Cobb and added, 'You like him, don't you?'

Did he? Cobb reluctantly supposed he did. 'Yeah, maybe, but I'd never ever let him know that!'